Middle Ages for the Classroom

Middle Ages for the Classroom

Plays, Fairy Tales and Resources for the Classroom Teacher

Eric Burnett and Joey DeStefanis

Writers Club Press
San Jose New York Lincoln Shanghai

Middle Ages for the Classroom
Plays, Fairy Tales and Resources for the Classroom Teacher

Writers Club Press
an imprint of iUniverse, Inc.

For information address:
iUniverse, Inc.
5220 S. 16th St., Suite 200
Lincoln, NE 68512
www.iuniverse.com

Any resemblance to actual people and events is purely coincidental.
This is a work of fiction.

ISBN: 0-595-23430-5

Printed in the United States of America

CONTENTS

A QUICK AND BLOODY HISTORY OF THE MIDDLE AGES

Joey DeStefanis

Kids love the Middle Ages because it is filled with battles, castles, and plagues. The following information highlights some important high interest events in the medieval timeline. I use these events as the backbone for my Middle Ages play and historical unit. Some of the website links are made for children and provide fun facts, while other sites provide more detailed information for adult audiences. All of the web links were current at the time of publication and, as always, adults should supervise children while surfing the Internet.

500 C.E (Common Era): The Middle Ages Begin.

Rome had been around for about a thousand years (Republic 510—31 B.C.E Empire 31 B.C—476 C.E) and had accomplished a LOT! They had an army that defeated pretty much everybody. They founded cities all over Europe (like London and Cologne). They built a fantastic system of aqueducts and roads and created the alphabet that most people in the western world still use today. It is important to emphasize to students how advanced the Romans were so they may understand why the Middle Ages is called "The Dark Ages!"

For more information check out these web sites:
http://www.roman-empire.net/
http://www.roman-empire.net/children/achieve.html

http://www.historyforkids.org/learn/romans/
http://www.bbc.co.uk/schools/romans/index.shtml
http://campus.northpark.edu/history/WebChron/Mediterranean/RomeR
ep.html
http://www.roman-empire.net/children/famous.html

500—1065: The Dark Ages!

Not a whole lot happened during this time. After Rome collapsed, most people left the cities and began to farm for a living. Even the great Forum of Rome became a place where farmers took their cattle to graze. Trading goods (the barter system) replaced Roman money. A new way of life called the feudal system began.

Most people in the Middle Ages formed small communities around a central lord or master. They lived on a manor, which usually had a castle or big house, the church, the village, and the surrounding farmland. These manors were isolated and self-sufficient. Basically they had everything they needed to survive and received few visitors. Most peasants never traveled more than a few miles from their home in their entire lifetime.

Peasants were poor people who worked for a Lord on the manor. In most parts of Europe, peasants made up over 90% of the population. They worked very hard for the Lord, and in return the Lord gave them small plots of land so they could grow their own food.

Other than peasants, there was the clergy and nobility. During the Middle Ages the Catholic Church was by far the biggest religion in Europe. Members of the clergy were considered very important during the Middle Ages.

The nobility were the privileged few who controlled the manors. More importantly, the nobles were the ones who became knights and fought in daring battles and went on magnificent quests!

For more information:
http://emuseum.mankato.msus.edu/history/middleages/
http://www.kyrene.k12.az.us/schools/brisas/sunda/ma/mahome.htm
http://www.learner.org/exhibits/middleages/feudal.html
http://www.historyforkids.org/learn/medieval/
http://www.kidskonnect.com/MiddleAges/MiddleAgesHome.html

To find about castles:
http://www.nationalgeographic.com/castles/enter.html
http://www.pbs.org/wgbh/nova/lostempires/trebuchet/destroy.html
http://www.castlesontheweb.com/
http://www.castles-of-britain.com/castle6.htm
http://www.inlandregion.org/SCA/misc/castle-parts.html

1066: The Battle of Hastings

A French duke, William of Normandy, wanted to be king of England. He thought he had a good claim to the throne because he was a cousin of a former king of England and he was married to an English noblewoman, Matilda of Flanders. Over in England, King Harold thought he should be king of England because, well, he was already King.

William loaded up longboats with men, horses, and armor. They crossed the channel and landed in England. William had one big advantage over Harold. He had men who fought on horseback called chevaliers, from the French word for horse *cheval*. The English army was mostly foot soldiers so the warriors on horseback were pretty scary to the

English. The battle took place on October 14, 1066. Two of Harold's brothers were killed and then Harold was struck in the face with an arrow. The Normans then broke through the English defense and killed Harold.

William was crowned King of England on Christmas Day in Westminister Abbey. He spent the rest of his life crushing revolts and then became known as William the Conqueror. Unfortunately for him, his death wasn't all that glorious. He died when his horse fell and crushed him!

The Battle of Hastings is important for a couple of reasons. First, it was the last time England was successfully invaded. A second reason is that due to William's interests in France (he was still the Duke of Normandy) England began to look beyond their own borders and became involved with events on the continent of Europe.

For more information:
http://members.tripod.com/~Battle_of_Hastings/Contents.html
http://www.battle1066.com/
http://www.infokey.com/hon/hastings.htm
http://www.bbc.co.uk/history/war/normans/hastings_01.shtml

1096—1291 The Crusades

Crusade means "war of the cross." Basically, Christians from all over Europe went to Jerusalem to "free" the home of Jesus from Muslims.

Before the official First Crusade was the Peasants' Crusade. A man named Peter the Hermit gathered up a mob of about 30,000 men to free Jerusalem. They did a lot of stupid things. They robbed and killed Jews as they passed through Germany and when they reached foreign lands they began killing local Christians because they thought they were Turks. When they finally arrived in the Holy Land, the Turks crushed the mob army and the survivors of Peter's army were sold into slavery.

The official First Crusade was a success. Pope Urban II promised all crusaders that they wouldn't be punished in purgatory, which means they would get to heaven quickly. With such a great offer, up to 60,000 men signed up for the Crusade. After months of travel and fighting, the Crusaders captured Jerusalem on July 15, 1099.

The Arabs and Turks did not like being ruled by the Christians and kept fighting to get their land back. The Turks fought so much that a Second Crusade was sent from Europe to stop them. It failed, because in 1187 the Turks recaptured Jerusalem.

Six more Crusades were sent to the Holy Land to recapture Jerusalem, but the Turks held on. It wasn't until over six hundred years later, in 1917, that the Turks lost control of Jerusalem.

For more information:
http://www.fordham.edu/halsall/sbook1k.html
http://www.medievalcrusades.com/
http://www.mrdowling.com/606islam.html

1215: Magna Carta

History has been mean to King John. Kids all over the world know him as the bad guy in Robin Hood, and he was forced to sign a famous scroll called the Magna Carta. John's older brother was the very popular King Richard. Richard was a hero because he helped capture Jerusalem during the crusades. So when John became king and lost a war with France (and a lot of French land), he looked very bad compared to the memory of his older brother. John also mad the Pope so angry he decided to close all the churches in England. Most Englishmen thought they would be doomed to Hell without going to church. So they were REALLY mad at King John. John invaded France and was badly beaten again. By this time the powerful Barons were really mad and drew up a list of complaints and demands.

In June 1215 King John met up with the barons at Runnymede to sign the Magna Carta. King John had to agree not to interfere with the church. He also couldn't imprison or sentence a person without a trial, and he couldn't raise taxes without consent from the nobles. The Magna Carta was the first step in taking absolute power away from the kings.

For more information:
http://www.fordham.edu/halsall/source/mcarta.html—The actual text online
http://www.historylearningsite.co.uk/magna_carta.htm
http://www.nara.gov/exhall/charters/magnacarta/magmain.html

1347—1350 The Plagues

The Black Death or Black Plague was a disaster. Some historians say that one out of every three people died and others say half the population or more died. The Black Death occurred towards the end of the Middle Ages when many people began to live in crowded cities. Sanitation was a big problem. People would use a chamber pot for a toilet and then throw their waste out the window and into the streets. Residents would also throw their trash into the streets. This was a great environment for rats and fleas, which carried the disease, but a very bad thing for the health of people. Villagers weren't safe from the plague either, and sometimes, entire villages were deserted as people died and moved away. The nursery rhyme Ring Around the Rosies is based on the symptoms of the plague.

For more information:
http://cybersleuth-kids.com/sleuth/History/Medieval/Black_Death/
http://www.rooneydesign.com/RingRosies.html
http://www.byu.edu/ipt/projects/middleages/LifeTimes/Plague.html

1381—The Peasants' Revolt

The Peasants' Revolt of 1381 took place in England. The peasants had always had a hard life, but during the plagues it only became worse. The Black Death killed so many people that many manors didn't have enough workers. Lords still expected all of the work to get done so this meant more work! In some cases, lords were so desperate for help they had granted their peasants freedom and paid them to work the land. Peasants liked their freedom and were prepared to fight to keep it. Meanwhile, wars with France were dragging on and costing a lot of money for the government, which meant more taxes had to be paid by the peasants.

Having more work and paying more taxes made the peasants receptive to the words of wandering priests who were preaching that all men should be equal. A man named John Ball made many popular speeches to peasants. He asked why the rich should be rich and the peasants poor when "we are all children of Adam and Eve?" Angry peasants decided not to pay taxes so collectors were sent out. In some villages tax collectors were beaten up and thrown in the duck pond. A mob of peasants from Essex and Kent began to march to London. Their leader was a man named Wat Tyler. On their way to London, the groups of peasants broke into houses and took food, although Wat Tyler and John Ball insisted that they paid for what they ate.

The army reached London and sympathizers inside the city opened the gates to them. The rebelling peasants destroyed homes of the rich and even hanged some people. They refused to leave until they met the young King Richard II. The peasants and the King met at Mile End and King Richard promised to make life better for the peasants. Everything was going well until they met again and the lord mayor killed Wat Tyler for an unknown reason. Well, then things didn't go well for the peasants. John Ball was killed, the revolt was crushed, and King Richard II didn't keep his promises. However, landowners learned a lesson and life for the peasants slowly improved.

For more information:
http://www.historylearningsite.co.uk/peasants_revolt.htm
http://www.britannia.com/history/articles/peasantsrevolt.html
http://www.britannia.com/history/docs/peasant.html

1500—Renaissance Begins

The Renaissance means rebirth. So what was being reborn? Greek and Roman ideals. In 1492 Columbus sailed to the "new world" and an age of discovery and learning began.

For more information:
http://www.learner.org/exhibits/renaissance/
http://web.uccs.edu/~history/index/renaissance.html

MIDDLE AGES TIMELINE

500   Beginning of Middle Ages (476 is official collapse of Rome)

1066   Battle of Hastings

1096–1291   Crusades

1215   Magna Carta

1347–1350   Black Plague (Plagues continued to appear afterwards)

1381   Peasants' Revolt

1500   Renaissance begins, Middle Ages ends

TALES OF KING D

Joey DeStefanis

Overview

My Middle Ages play has three components: A chronological journey from the fall of Rome to the onset of the Renaissance, two legends of King Arthur, and the grand finale King D and the Siege of the Really Rottens. Our first act begins in 476 where we witness the fall of ancient Rome and the dawn of the Middle Ages. In the second act, a young boy named Arthur manages to pull a sword out of a stone and becomes king. King Arthur, Merlin, and the Knights of the Round Table then spring into action in the First Quest of the Round table. The Battle of Hastings is the first of our historical Middle Ages events. William of Normandy defeats King Harold with the help of his chevaliers and is crowned king on Christmas day. Next we get a brief report on the Crusades from King Richard and learn about the Magna Carta. King John complains miserably, but the nobles and narrators tell us why the Magna Carta is a great document. The Black Plagues disrupt everyday life and the peasants decide to throw tax collectors in the duck pond during the Peasants' Revolt. The grand finale of our play is King D and the Siege of the Really Rottens. King D, the kindest, wisest, and most handsome king in all the land, is getting old and needs an heir. Prince Handsome is ready to rule, but he has an unfortunate crush on the unpopular Princess Picky. Meanwhile, Sir Really Rotten and his Really Rottens decide to siege King D's castle. Although Lady Lovely and Sir Whines-A-Lot try to deter Sir Really Rotten from attacking, a wild battle rages on to decide ownership of the castle and manor.

Total Parts: 56 plus

Lead Characters:

King Arthur
Merlin
King John
King D
Prince Handsome
Princess Picky
Sir Really Rotten
Sir Whines-A-Lot
Lady Lovely

Large Speaking Roles

19 Narrators

Minor Roles

Town Crier
Slave
Senator Smarticus
Caesar
Roman Guards
Barbarians
Strong Knight #1
Strong Knight #2
Sir Giant
Sir Ector
Sir Kay

King Utherpendragon
Sir Gawain
Sir Abelleus
Sir Tor
White Hart (Deer)
Lady
Stranger Knight
Lord of the Castle
William the Conqueror (Large acting role, but no speaking)
King Harold
King Richard (Large one-time speaking role)
Three Nobles
Four Children
Tax Collector
King D's Peasants
Castle Defenders
Really Rotten Castle Attackers

INTRODUCTION AND ROME

CAST:

Town Crier
Narrator One
Narrator Two
Narrator Three
Caesar
Senator Smarticus
Slave
Roman Guards (non speaking part)
Barbarians (grunting only)

NARRATOR ONE: Lords and ladies, welcome to our class presentation of the Middle Ages—also known as the dark ages and medieval times. What do those names mean you might be wondering and what happened during that time? Well today we're going to perform some skits that tell you about the history and legends of the Middle Ages. Enjoy!

TOWN CRIER: (Yells) Act One: Ancient Rome

NARRATOR TWO: Ancient Rome: The year is 476. Rome, the largest empire the world has ever known, is falling apart:

SLAVE: Hail Caesar!

Caesar enters room in toga, waves to the people, and sits on his throne.

CAESAR: Ah Senator Smarticus, what say you?

SENATOR SMARTICUS: (stands by Caesar's side—also in toga): "Caesar, those barbarians from the north are attacking our borders again. (*Three students dressed as barbarians kill two students dressed as roman guards*) We really ought to send out more armies!"

Caesar: "Hah! Rome has been around for a 1,000 years! Do you really think barbarians could end our glorious civilization? We have brought the world its greatest roads and buildings. We have great scholars and magnificent libraries. We are the most advanced civilization the world has ever known—why should we worry about barbarians?"

Three barbarians rush in and kill Caesar and Senator Smarticus.

Lights in room are turned off.

NARRATOR THREE: Just like that the glorious empire of Rome crumbled and the Dark Ages began. Why is it called the Dark Ages? Well, the great cities and centers of learning were destroyed. The great forum of Rome—the capital of the empire—became a place where farmers took their cows to eat wheat and grass. People left the open trade of the cities and towns to live in manors protected by castles and walls.

ACT 2: THE LEGENDS OF KING ARTHUR

CAST

PART 1: THE SWORD IN THE STONE

Town Crier
Narrator One
Narrator Two
Narrator Three
Strong Knight #1
Strong Knight #2
Sir Giant
Young Arthur
Sir Ector
Sir Kay

PART 2: THE FIRST QUEST OF THE ROUND TABLE

Town Crier
Narrator One
Narrator Two
Narrator Three
King Arthur
Merlin
King Utherpendragon
Sir Gawain
Sir Abelleus
Sir Tor
White Hart (Deer)
Lady
Stranger Knight
Lord of the Castle

TOWN CRIER: (*yells*) Act 2 Part 1: The Sword in the Stone

NARRATOR ONE: Our class would now like to perform some legends about King Arthur's Camelot. These stories take place in England a long time ago, before William the Conqueror came to the land. Our first story is about how King Arthur became King.

NARRATOR TWO: King Utherpendragon was a powerful king who had a son that was one day going to be King Arthur. But the son didn't know anything about himself because the King had baby Arthur taken away by Merlin the magician for safekeeping. Merlin sent young Arthur to live with Sir Ector, and he and his wife were very good parents to Arthur.

NARRATOR THREE: After a while the King died and there was a lot of fighting in the land. So Merlin asked for all the Lords of England to gather on Christmas day to pick a king. When they got there they found a giant stone with a sword stuck in it. The words on the stone said: "Whoso Pulleth out this sword of this stone and anvil is rightwise King born of England."

STRONG KNIGHT #1: "Wow! All I got to do is pull this sword out and I'm king! No problem." (Knight struggles but can't pull sword out)

STRONG KNIGHT #2: "Move over Sir Wimpy I'm the true king of England!" (*Knight pulls and pulls but can't budge sword*)

NARRATOR ONE: Many, many knights tried their best to pull out the sword but none could move it even a millimeter! But then the biggest and most powerful knight in all the lands marched his way to the stone.

STRONG KNIGHT #1: "Look! It's Sir Giant!"

KNIGHTS: Oooh! Ahhhhhh!

SIR GIANT: Out of my way puny children or I will squish you like grapes! Now I become King! (*Sir giant struggles and struggles but can't budge sword*). Oh no, I think I hear my mommy calling!

NARRATOR TWO: After Sir Giant ran home to his mommy a great tournament began. Arthur was there to help his big brother Sir Kay.

SIR KAY: Arthur I can't find my sword. Go back to our tent and get me another one.

ARTHUR: Okay.

NARRATOR THREE: Arthur rode back to the tent, but he couldn't find the sword.

ARTHUR: Oh no! I can't find a sword my brother will kill me! (*Turns and sees sword in the stone*) Oh here's a sword. I'll take that one. (*Arthur grabs the sword with one hand and gallops to Sir Kay*} Here you go.

SIR KAY: Thanks. (*He looks at sword shocked!*) Father! Father! Look I am the true king of England I pulled out the sword!

Arthur looks surprised. He has no idea what Sir Kay is talking about.

SIR ECTOR (*stares hard at sir Kay*): Do you really expect me to believe that?

SIR KAY: Oh all right, Arthur did it. He is the true king!

Now a crowd of knights has gathered to hear this amazing story. Soon they all gallop back to the stone.

SIR ECTOR: Okay Arthur put the sword back in and then pull it out.

(*Arthur puts the sword in, but then strong knight #1 rushes in and grabs it. But he can't pull it out. Then Arthur brushes him aside, grabs the sword with one hand, and pulls it out*).

EVERYONE: (the people kneel and shout): "All hail the king!"

ACT TWO PART TWO—THE FIRST QUEST OF THE ROUND TABLE

NARRATOR ONE: Our next play is all about the First Quest of the Round Table and the meaning of chivalry.

Four knights gather around a rectangle table and start fighting:

SIR GAWAIN:	"I want to be closest to King Arthur"
SIR ABELLEUS:	"No I do!"
SIR TOR:	"I'm not going to be at the low end"
KING PELLINORE:	"Hey I'm older"
SIR GAWAIN:	"I'm a better knight!"

MERLIN (*shaking his head*): Stop fighting! We shall have a round table to solve this problem. At a round table all are equal because there is no high and low end.

Everyone sits at round table.

KING ARTHUR: Well knights I guess we need to go on a quest or something.

MERLIN: Behold! An adventure is coming.

(*A white hart (deer) runs through the room. Behind it is a dog. The dog knocks over Sir Abelleus who gets up and takes the dog away with him. Then a lady comes running into the room*)

LADY: My lord King suffer me not to be robbed! That dog is mine that yonder knight has taken away!

KING ARTHUR: (*shaking his head*) Really this doesn't seem to be any of our business lady.

(*Then a stranger knight rides into room and takes away lady*).

KING ARTHUR: Phew! Glad that's over. Now...

MERLIN: King Arthur! You must not take this lightly. Such an adventure must be followed to the end.

ARTHUR: Oh okay. I was hoping to fight a dragon or something for our first quest.

MERLIN: This is more important! Send Sir Gawain to get the white hart. Send Sir Tor to get the dog and our knight. And then let king Pellinore go get the lady and the bad knight. When they get back I will have an important lesson for everyone.

NARRATOR TWO: The three knights were excited for adventure and they hurried off for their quest. Sir Gawain chased the white hart for a long time. Finally the white hart entered a castle. Dogs inside the castle killed the white hart! The Lord of the Castle was very angry!

LORD: That's the white hart I gave to my lady. A cruel death to these dogs!

SIR GAWAIN: Cease from this! Fight me instead.

NARRATOR THREE: After a fierce battle Sir Gawain wounded the Lord of the Castle badly.

LORD: Oh please don't kill me. Please pretty please you kind knight you!

SIR GAWAIN: Hah! You shall die!

NARRATOR ONE: Sir Gawain angrily lifted his sword and he meant to cut off the lord's head! But at that moment the lady of the castle ran into the room and flung herself on her husband's body. Unable to stop, Sir Gawain cut off the lady's head instead!

SIR GAWAIN: Oh no this is terrible. I am a shamed knight now.

NARRATOR TWO: Sir Gawain sadly rode back to Camelot. Meanwhile Sir Tor had finally found the dog. Then Sir Abelleus, who had left King Arthur's round table with the dog, saw Sir Tor holding the dog and said:

SIR ABELLEUS: Hey! Give me back that dog. It's mine now!

NARRATOR THREE: Without saying a word, Sir Tor got set to fight Sir Abelleus. After a mighty battle Sir Abelleus was lying on the ground in pain.

SIR TOR: Yield now!

SIR ABELLEUS: Never! Not until I get that dog back!

SIR TOR: The dog is going back to King Arthur!

NARRATOR ONE: Sir Tor killed Sir Abelleus and then was returning to Camelot when he found King Pellinore who was very sad.

SIR TOR: Alas, what is wrong?

KING PELLINORE: The shame is mine. I was so caught up in my quest that I didn't stop to save a damsel in distress. Soon after I learned an evil knight killed her. But I didn't save her because all I could think about was my quest.

NARRATOR TWO: Soon all the knights returned to the round table where Merlin had an important lesson for everyone:

MERLIN: Knights! I lay upon you all the order of Chivalry. Sir Gawain didn't give mercy to the lord of the castle and now he will be haunted by the memory of the dead lady for all his days. Sir Abelleus was not loyal and acted selfishly, taking the dog for himself and leaving our company. In the end, death will come to the selfish and greedy. King Pellinore didn't stop to help a lady in need. Always give all the help in your power to ladies. And never, on pain of death and eternal disgrace, do anything bad to a woman.
You must promise to do three things: You must always be kind. You must always tell the truth, and you must always help other people.

NARRATOR THREE: And so now you know how the round table and chivalry came to be about!

ACT THREE: THE BATTLE OF HASTINGS

CAST

Town Crier
Narrator One
Narrator Two
Narrator Three
William the Conqueror
King Harold

TOWN CRIER: (*yells*) Act 3: The Battle of Hastings.

NARRATOR ONE: 1066 is one of the most famous dates in history. It was the last time anyone had ever successfully invaded England.

NARRATOR TWO: This is William of Normandy. (*Audience: hurray!*) He felt he should be king of England because he was the cousin of a former King and married to Matilda of Flanders.

NARRATOR THREE: This is King Harold. (*Audience boos.*)

KING HAROLD (*interrupts*): Hey I am King of England! Why do these history books make me out to be the bad guy? Normandy's in France you know?

NARRATOR ONE: Well anyway, while in France, William created a navy of boats and loaded them with soldiers and horses. The Normans had a special group of fighters called the chevaliers, from the French word cheval, meaning horse. The chevaliers fought on horseback, which was a very strange and scary way of fighting to the English who almost always fought on foot!

NARRATOR TWO: The battle took place on October 14, 1066. King Harold was waiting on top of a hill. William and the Normans charged up the hill but were repelled by the English over and over again. The fighting was so bloody they say the hill was slick from blood.

NARRATOR THREE: Two of King Harold's brothers were slain. Still the English fought on. Suddenly, King Harold was struck in the face with an arrow and the wound put his eye out! With their King writhing in pain, the English were disheartened and the Normans broke through the lines and killed King Harold!

NARRATOR ONE: With the King dead the English ran and William became know as William the Conqueror! William was crowned king of England on Christmas Day in Westminster Abbey. Ever since then the royal crown of England has been passed down from one king or queen to another without any invasions until this very day!

NARRATOR TWO: William spent the rest of his life conquering the rest of England. He died at the age of 50, not in battle, but when his horse fell and crushed him!

NARRATOR THREE: The Battle of Hastings was recorded on the Bayeux tapestry, which we are lucky enough to have the original copy here! (*Students present a hand drawn version of the battle events to the audience*)

ACT 4: MAGNA CARTA

CAST

Narrator One
Narrator Two
Narrator Three
King Richard
King John
The Three Nobles

TOWN CRIER: (*yells*) Act 4:Magna Carter

NARRATOR ONE: Poor King John. Nobody liked him when he was alive, and he still gets made fun of today. How many of you have seen Walt Disney's Robin Hood? Well, King John is the wimpy lion that always did rotten things. Except then he was Prince John. His brother Richard was King while the Robin Hood stories took place. You see King Richard wasn't around because he was fighting in the Crusades. Right King Richard?

KING RICHARD: That's right narrator. The Crusades means War of the Cross. I was off to save Jerusalem, the home of our lord Jesus Christ, from the Turks. The land where Jesus lived and preached was also home to people of two other great religions, the Jews and the Muslims. All three of our religions wanted to own that land and during the Middle Ages Christians all over Europe set out to win it in battle. We were successful for many years, but shortly before I died The Turks recaptured Jerusalem in 1187 and held on to the land for the next 730 years!

NARRATOR TWO: Thank you King Richard. And now back to your miserable little brother John.

KING JOHN: You know I really don't think this is fair.

NARRATOR THREE: Why not? Your eating habits were disgusting.

KING JOHN: So was everyone else's.

NARRATOR ONE: You stuffed yourself with food until you couldn't move and drank yourself senseless.

KING JOHN: Can't a king have any fun?

NARRATOR TWO: Humph. King John had a nephew named Arthur— not King Arthur. Philip of France thought John was treating the boy badly and war broke out.

KING JOHN: My nephew was a brat.

NARRATOR THREE: And at the beginning of the war you took him pris- oner! Phillip won the war and took most of king John's French land away. Needless to say this didn't make him very popular with the nobles in England!

NOBLES: Not at all!

NARRATOR ONE: Then King John quarreled with the Pope who promptly closed all the churches in England! This was a disaster to the very religious people of the middle ages and they thought they wouldn't get into heaven! The pope even asked King Philip of France to invade England! John decided to make peace with the pope and pay him money.

KING JOHN: Nobody's perfect

NARRATOR TWO: Well then King John decided to invade France and he lost again! This time the powerful nobles were angry!

NOBLES: Your wars have cost us a lot of money in taxes and good land! England gets weaker by the day with you on the throne!

KING JOHN: Oh sure blame everything on me.

NARRATOR THREE: The nobles drew up a list of complaints and threatened to attack his castles and estates. They wanted to have some say in how the country was run.

NOBLES: Yeah!

NARRATOR ONE: The King met up with the most powerful nobles at Runnymede in 1215 to sign a very famous document called the Magna Carta.

KING JOHN: A terrible document!

NOBLES: A great document!

NARRATOR TWO: In signing the Magna Carta, King John agreed not to interfere with the church and never to imprison or sentence a man without a trial. He also couldn't raise taxes without the consent of the nobles. The Magna Carta was the first step in taking absolute power away from the Kings.

KING JOHN: How sad.

NOBLES: How great!

ACT 5: THE BLACK PLAGUE AND PEASANT'S REVOLT!

CAST

Narrator One
Narrator Two
Narrator Three
Four Children
Tax Collector

TOWN CRIER: (*yells*) Act 5: The Black Plague and Peasants' Revolt!

NARRATOR ONE: Has anyone ever heard the nursery rhyme: Ring around the rosies pocket full of posies, ashes to ashes we all fall down! Well this rhyme is actually about the bubonic plague or Black Death! England and the rest of Europe had many plagues during the Middle Ages and even some after. Most people think this nursery rhyme was actually written for plagues that happened in the 1600's. But whenever it was written, the meaning of the lines is the same:

NARRATOR TWO: Ring around the rosies meant that a rash of red bumps formed around the eyes.

CHILD #1: "Oh no! Look at your face!"

CHILD #2: "My face my beautiful face!

NARRATOR THREE: Pocket full of posies means a pocket full of flowers—people thought flowers would keep the plague away from them because many people thought the plague was spread through bad odors.

CHILD #3: "Good thing I have these flowers to keep _____'s bad smell away."

NARRATOR ONE: Ashes, ashes—meant so many people were dying that sometimes people burned the clothes of the dead bodies to stop the spread of the horrible smell. Sometimes the rhyme uses "a tishoo a tishoo" which means that sneezing was one of the last symptoms before you...

A child sneezes and then CHILD #4: (*shouts*) "Oh no! She's going to..."

NARRATOR TWO: Die!—Which is the "We all fall down" part.—It also meant that everyone died and in England as many as one out of every three people died from the plague—so to them it seemed like everyone was going to die soon!

NARRATOR THREE: The Black Death happened near the end of the Middle Ages. When one out of three people die it is a shock to normal life. There were not enough people to work the fields and England kept fighting wars with France. On top of all of this the king decided to raise taxes!

TAX COLLECTOR: "Hey you dirty peasants! You better pay me your taxes!"

NARRATOR ONE: Wandering priests also started preaching that all men should be equal. They would say, "What makes the rich think they are better than you? We are all children of Adam and Eve. How did he get rich at our expense?

NARRATOR TWO: A lot of peasants agreed and decided not to pay taxes. When the king's tax collectors came they were beaten up and thrown in the duck pond! (*Tax collector is thrown into pond*).

NARRATOR THREE: King Richard II fought back, but he also promised the peasants a better life. Slowly, the peasant way of life began to disappear, but it took a very long time.

THE GRAND FINALE: KING D AND THE SIEGE OF THE REALLY ROTTENS

CAST

Narrator

King D
Prince Handsome
Princess Picky
Peasants
Sir Really Rotten

Sir Whines A Lot

Lady Lovely
Castle Defenders
Really Rotten Castle Attackers

NARRATOR: Here we are at the magnificent Castle D, home to King D, the kindest, wisest, and most handsome king in all the land. He had bravely slain three dragons, smote 47 evil enemies, and won the National Chess Challenge seven times.

Dramatic entrance music should accompany the King's entrance. Also Sprach Zarathustra (Them from 2001: A Space Odyssey) works best.

KING D: Oh peasants! Because I am so benevolent, I will give you all one extra turnip for dinner!

PEASANTS: Oh thank you! Thank you my kind lord! All hail Lord D! You are too kind!

KING D: Yes, it's true I am too kind. But you know you peasants do work the fields that produce my food, and you provided the labor that built my castle, and you were the ones who were in the front lines dying during all my wars that made me the rich wonderful guy I am today, so you really do deserve that extra turnip!

PEASANTS: Oh no! No! We love doing all of your work! You are too kind.

NARRATOR: Unfortunately, Lord D was now the decrepit old age of 31 and his dashing son, Prince Handsome, was ready to take the throne.

PEASANTS: (Cheering the arrival of Prince Handsome). What a hunk! He's so charming!

PRINCE HANDSOME: Father! I am ready to rule! I have it all: fantastic good looks, brilliant brains, and a really great smile. But I am missing one thing.

LORD D: Humility?

PRINCE HANDSOME: No! I need a wife! Someone to be my Queen when I take the throne. Beauty is still sleeping, Cinderella ran away with Charming, and I don't even want to talk about Snow White and those seven dwarfs! It seems the only available "Royal" material is Princess Picky.

PEASANTS (booing arrival of Princess Picky): What a snob! She's so mean!

PRINCESS PICKY: Like anyone cares what you peasants think anyway! Why don't you all go burn your clothes and take a bath? My royal nose hairs are burning from your putrid smell!

LORD D: Son, there's a lot to be said for the bachelor's life.

PRINCE HANDSOME: No father, I must be a model king and take a proper blue—blooded royal wife! Princess Picky will you—

PEASANTS: No! No! Don't do it! Save yourself! Save us!

PRINCE HANDSOME: Will you marry me?

PRINCESS PICKY: It's about time you asked!

PRINCE HANDSOME: So you'll marry me?

PRINCESS PICKY: Well it took you forever to ask, so you're obviously not very smart. You haven't killed your father yet, so you're not very ambitious. You don't torture your peasants like any sensible Lord would, so you're not very ruthless. And your teeth are just a tad crooked, so you're smile's not really that great either. Hmmmm. I'll have to think about it. (*She storms off into the keep*).

PRINCE HANDSOME (*excited*): I think she likes me! I'm going to get married!

NARRATOR: Meanwhile, unbeknownst to the good people, well mostly good people, of Castle D, the really rotten knight Sir Really Rotten was swiftly marching towards Castle D.

SIR REALLY ROTTEN: Ha! Ha! Ha! This is my greatest rotten plan yet! I will siege King D's castle, kill the old fool, throw his goody two shoe handsome son in the dungeon, and work those lazy peasants 'till they die! With my great weapons and army of peasant pawns they won't have a chance of stopping me! Ha! Ha! Ha!

NARRATOR: Sir Really Rotten had captured the well-loved Lady Lovely and she was forced to go on this awful mission.

LADY LOVELY: Oh really, Rotten why do you have to be so greedy? You already have six castles and more money than you can spend in 20 lifetimes, what's the point?

SIR REALLY ROTTEN: What's the point? What's the point! Give me a break lady; it's power and glory I'm after! You can never have too many castles!

NARRATOR: All of Sir Really Rotten's army were mean and greedy soldiers who loved to fight. All except Sir Really Rotten's trusty advisor: Sir Whines A Lot

SIR WHINES A LOT: Oh sir I'm really worried, you do know it's almost impossible to siege a castle? I mean with the moat and barbican and—

SIR REALLY ROTTEN: Details! Details! I'm sure it can't be that tough with old man Lord D in charge.

NARRATOR: Soon Really Rotten's men, and Lady Lovely, were outside the walls of Castle D and the siege was on!

PEASANTS: Oh no! Our castle is being invaded! This is horrible!

KING D: Hah! Not to fear my lowly ones. As you soon will see a castle is almost impossible to break into!

REALLY ROTTEN: Almost is right! But soon you will see that sometimes it happens!

NARRATOR: The first obstacle was the moat.

ROTTEN INVADER #1: I know! I'll swim across! (*starts to drown*) Help! Help! My 50 pounds of armor is drowning me! (*invader drowns and his hit with arrows from above*).

SIR WHINES A LOT: It's all over! Let's turn back!

SIR REALLY ROTTEN: We've got a siege tower. We'll be over that wall in time for lunch!

SIR WHINES A LOT: Oh those things never work!

NARRATOR: The Really Rotten bad guys moved the siege tower to Castle D's wall, but the defenders set it ablaze with flaming arrows and Greek fire.

KING D: Ha! Where'd you get that siege tower Rotten? Toys R US?

SIR REALLY ROTTEN: (*Waves fists angrily*) Laugh it up while you can geezer!

SIR WHINES A LOT: Sir, the walls are too thick to break and too well guarded to climb. We only have three options. One: Starve them out— which means we'll be sitting here for a long time and they might send reinforcements to surround us. Two: we can dig a tunnel underneath the wall, set the support beams on fire, and hope the wall collapses. Three: Our best chance. Send a spy in and get him to open that drawbridge for us!

SIR REALLY ROTTEN: Let's send that spy!

Rotten spy sneaks into castle

NARRATOR: Meanwhile, Princess Picky was awoken from her afternoon nap by all the commotion.

PRINCESS PICKY: Oh brother, we're being invaded. This is just great. I had to yell at 12 peasants and whip three servants today and now I suppose I won't be able to take my evening gallop in the forest.

PRINCE HANDSOME: Dear, can't you see we're being invaded! We've got more important things to do!

PRINCESS PICKY: You're right! I must make sure we cut the peasants food rations in half. If this is going to last a while I can't be expected to suffer you know!

NARRATOR: Meanwhile, the Rotten spy had snuck in through the postern gate—which is a hidden gate—and was able to open the drawbridge!

SIR REALLY ROTTEN: Ha! Ha! Now the castle is ours!

PRINCE HANDSOME: A spy! Throw him in the dungeon and—

PRINCESS PICKY: Oh no the dungeon's full, just throw him in the moat! (*she kicks spy into the moat*) Guards lower the barbican! (*Princess is safely inside*).

KING D: Nice Try Rotten, but you'll never get through our barbican gate!

SIR REALLY ROTTEN: Knights charge the barbican, I'm going to rip that guys sideburns off!

LADY LOVELY: Really, this is sooooo unnecessary! The population is low, food and land is plenty, why can't we all just share the land and live in peace and harmony?

REALLY ROTTEN: You are so weird! Knights, remind me to have her locked in the dungeon when we get inside.

Fierce fighting takes place with warriors dying on both sides. Finally, the barbican is broken and two Rotten soldiers rush through only to:

PRINCE HANDSOME (dropping boulders): Ha! Take that!

ROTTEN KNIGHTS (*Screaming together*): Oh no! The murder holes!

NARRATOR: After passing the barbican, the Rotten attackers had to pass under the deadly murder holes. King D's defenders dropped boulders on their head and boiling water!

KING D: Time to take a bath baby!

Rotten Knights jump in moat screaming.

SIR WHINES A LOT: We're doomed! Even if we get past the murder holes we still have to break down the portcullis! All of our men our dying we're doomed! Doomed I say! Turn back –

Sir Whines A Lot is hit with arrows and dies very slowly, whining the whole time.

SIR REALLY ROTTEN: Phew! Am I glad he's dead!

PRINCESS PICKY: This is horrible, just horrible! All of my servants are off defending the castle and no one is free to rub the warts on my feet. This castle better hold up Handsome, or I'm definitely finding another husband!

The battle rages on and The Really Rotten attackers are killed with arrows and objects dropped through the murder holes.

NARRATOR: After a long battle, only a few of Really Rotten's men survived. King D, seeing Rotten's weakness, lowered the portcullis and rushed his men out to finish off the enemy!

LORD D: Let's get those rotten baddies!

NARRATOR: Soon, the extremely handsome King D and his trusty followers captured Rotten and his men.

PEASANTS: Hurray! All hail the king!

KING D: Thank you very much. Taking care of business is my motto baby.

SIR REALLY ROTTEN: You've won this time King D, but I'll be back soon with an even bigger and more rotten army! I'll have you drawn and quartered and used as lawn decorations.

PRINCESS PICKY: Wow! I like his style!

PRINCE HANDSOME: Lady Lovely, what are you doing with this buffoon?

LADY LOVELY: Sir Really Rotten captured me when I was teaching bible verses to the blind. Oh please free me from his evil clutches so that I may continue to help the poor and sick throughout out our great land.

REALLY ROTTEN: I think I'm gonna puke!

PRINCESS PICKY: Me too!

PRINCE HANDSOME: Oh my noble Lady Lovely, I shall free you at once! My dream is too open a health spa for victims of the black plague and turn the armory into a library for poor peasant children.

SIR REALLY ROTTEN: Cut off my ears! I can't take it anymore!

PRINCESS PICKY: That's it Handsome, there's no way I'm marrying a little sissy boy like you!

King D, Handsome, and Lady Lovely huddle together.

LORD D: Rotten, we have decided your punishment. It may be severe, but terrible acts call for terrible punishments.

PRINCE HANDSOME: Sir Really Rotten, by royal proclamation your punishment is you must marry Princess Picky!

SIR REALLY ROTTEN: Oh no! What about a 100 lashes! Running the gauntlet!

PRINCESS PICKY: Oh be quiet Rotten we've got a lot of work to do if I'm going to be Queen of England anytime soon!

PRINCE HANDSOME: Lady Lovely will you

PEASANTS: Awwwwwwwwwwww.

PRINCE HANDSOME: Will you marry me?

LADY LOVELY: Yes!

KING D: This is great! You know guys I've learned something today. Sir Really rotten has really rotten breath, and Love conquers all. You know the Renaissance is coming soon and I think it's time we all stopped this gloomy castle fighting nonsense and started talking about our feelings.

ALL ACTORS: Feelings! Nothing more than feelings!

NARRATOR: Around 1500 a period called the Renaissance began. Instead of building giant lonely castles, people began to build open cities and explore around the world. It was a time of discovery and learning. The Middle Ages ended and so does our play!

THE END

A Shining Star in a Dark Age

Eric Burnett

Overview

Medieval Europe is suffering through the worst of the Black Death. Children are suffering greatly and one young lady takes advantage of a unique twist of fate. One day, a young girl named Michaela is met in the forest by a wizard named Merlion who promises to alter her life if she simply accepts his magical belt. Michaela ends up changing bodies and her status when she touches a boy, Page Patrick. Michaela then journeys off and witnesses her first joust and the capture of Lady Purity. When no one else steps up to save the helpless victim, Michaela vows to save Lady Purity. After successfully defeating the dreaded Sir Fearful, Michaela goes on to become lord of the manor under the guise of being Sir Patrick. When Michaela's true identity is uncovered, the villagers are faced with a choice—suffer at the hands of their new lord or battle to return a woman to the throne.

Total Parts: 45

Lead Characters

Michaela
Cyrdon Siegeman
Gunther
Sir Sarcasticine
Sir Fearful

Merlion
Patrick

Minor Characters

Narrators 1 through 10
Peasants 1 through 11
Michael
William
Frederick
Romeo
Margaret
Lucy
Susan
Page Donald
Page Mailes
Lady Purity
Herald
Sir Valiant
Tunneler
Trebucheter
Battering Rammer
Damsel in Distress
Vanna

Scene 1

Narrator #1
Michael—36 year old father
William—17 year old son
Frederick—14 year old son
Romeo—11 year old son
Margaret—9 year old daughter
Michaela—8 year old son

Narrator: It is the year 1340 and the Black Plague has swept across Europe for the past two years, wiping out the population. People are dieing left and right. Some are even dieing vertically. The Gould family is gathered around their father, Michael, as he lays in bed, close to death.

William: (*shaking father*) Father, Father, can you hear me?

Romeo: He doesn't look too good. (*Turns to William*) Are cheeks supposed to be blue?

Frederick: You know, we shouldn't be looking at him. We could catch it too just by looking at him.

Romeo: Yeah, but he is our dad. What can we do? Have we tried everything?

Frederick: Everything the doctor told us.

Margaret: Did we shave a chicken's bottom?

Frederick: Yep...tried it...failed.

Romeo: Throw herbs on the fire?

Frederick: Yep...tried it...failed.

Romeo: Drill a hole in his head?

Frederick: Nope...Dad wasn't too excited when I explained the procedure.

Michaela: Did you kill all the cats and dogs in town?

Frederick: Most of them, but...the...uh...neighbors starting getting a bit upset.

Michaela: How did he catch this anyway?

Romeo: Gee, I don't know. Maybe he shouldn't be sleeping with Fluffy the Plague Carrying Rat.

Frederick: I've got it. He should sleep in the sewer. The smell of the drains will definitely kill the disease!

Margaret: Wow, that's a great idea. In fact, these are all great ideas. We sure have a lot of common sense in the Middle Ages.

Michael: No...(*grasping up at Romeo*)...keep me out of the drains. Fe...ces equals di...sease.

William: Father, it's me, William. Can you hear me? (*yells louder*) Can you hear me?

Michael: (*muttering at a half whisper while shivering*) Yes...my...son. I hear you. You're yelling at me.

William: Father, if you should not make it what will we do?

Michael: The...land is yours, my son. You must...now...raise the family.

William: Raise the family? I am barely a man. I don't even shave yet. How can I raise this family all alone? Mother died of the plague last harvest and we have survived on water and vegetables for over a year. If we don't get some food from the top of the food pyramid soon, we will surely die.

Michael: Send your...brothers away to the monastery or...to an..a..a..apren

William: Apprenticeship? Monastery? That will work for Frederick and Romeo, but what of Michaela and Margaret?

Michael: Margaret is 11 now. She is old enough to marry (coughing). Michaela...well...she will need to learn to survive.

William, Frederick and Romeo bend over to comfort their father. Margaret and Michaela walk to the side to talk privately.

Margaret: Did you hear that? Dad wants me to get married.

Michaela: Well, you are 11. It's not like you're getting any younger.

Margaret: Yeah, I was just happy I made it to eleven. After Robert, Thomas, Kimberly, Susan, Joyce, Sporky and Michael Jr. died, I wasn't feeling too good about my chances.

Michaela: So what…you have to get married. What am I going to do? The oldest son gets everything. You can at least get married. I might as well be dead.

Margaret: Michaela, don't say that! (*shakes Michaela*) The angel of death might just grant your wish and then…

Michael: (*coughing violently*)

Margaret and Mitchell return to their father's bedside.

Michael: (*continues coughing*) Goodbye children. I…loved you all…obviously William the best…but I loved you all

Michael Dies

Scene 2

William
Frederick
Michaela
Lucy—7 year old girl
Susan—7 year old girl
Merlion—Evil sorcerer

Lucy and Susan are outside playing a children's game. When Michaela hears the song, she runs out to stop them.

Susan and Lucy (*singing*): Ring around the rosey, pocket full of poseys, ashes, ashes, we all fall down. (*fall down*)

Lucy: Let's do it again! Let's do it again! That was a hoot!

Susan: OK, that would be swell.

Susan and Lucy (*singing*): Ring around the rosey—

Michaela: Stop it! Do you have no respect for the dead?

Susan: Golly gee willickers Michaela. It's just a song.

Michaela: Yeah…a song about death and all of us falling down. Well. My father just became one of the ashes.

Susan: Gee wiz Michaela. Why do you always have to analyze the song lyrics? It takes all the fun out of it.

Lucy: Oh Michaela. I'm sorry. I know it is hard when your family dies. I used to have eight sisters, or was it nine? No...there was Nancy. Wait...yeah nine. There was nine. But now, I'm down to just Susan.

Susan: If this Black Plague doesn't stop soon, I'm not going to have anyone to dance with and sing the rosey song.

Michaela: Could you please play somewhere else at least?

The girls walk away and continue their song. Michaela walks back towards his cottage and overhears her brother talking.

Frederick: We can't just kill her. She's our sister.

William: In my eyes, she is simply another mouth to feed.

Frederick: How can you say that?

William: Father told me that I'm in charge now and I say we take Michaela into the forest and...

Michaela: Oh no! They're going to kill me!

Just then they see Michaela looking in the door. A tear is falling down her face. She turns and runs away.

Frederick: Michaela, wait. We can explain. Michaela!!!

Michaela runs down the street and into the forest. After her exhaustion catches up to her, she sits down next to a tree and starts crying. A man dressed in an elaborate costume walks up to her.

Merlion: Child, why doth thou sheddeth tears in thy forest of discontent?

Michaela: Wha…what? What did you say?

Merlion: Twas curious that a young lady sheddeth tears so far from her manor. Thy problem tis unbeknownst to me. I sayeth again. Why doth thou sheddeth tears?

Michaela: Uhhh…buddy…why doth thou use the word "doth"? Can't you speak normal?

Merlion: Tis normal my speech. Tis you that speaketh with a wicked tongue.

Michaela: Who are you?

Merlion: Merlion tis my name. Granting wishes to ignorant children…like you…tis my game.

Michaela: Merlion? Don't you mean Merlin?

Merlion: Ye, tis true. Merlin tis a member of my brethren. However, his deeds in Camelot…can't stand the place…do not concern me. If thou follows my lead thy troubles shalt vanish like a cabbage before supper.

Michaela: Huh? Like a cabbage before supper?

Merlion: Focus not on my choice of simile. Focus on what I can giveth to thee. If thou wish, my offer of assistance shalt continue. Taketh this belt and your world will change forever.

Michaela: Why would I take your belt? You are a stranger.

Merlion: (*shocked and surprised*) Tis I a stranger? Thou thinketh suspicious thoughts. What harm cometh to you if you accept my gift? Tis your life perfect at the moment? Or tis your life in need of assistance?

Michaela: You have a point. I've definitely had better days. OK…I'll take your belt.

Merlion passes belt to Michaela.

Merlion: Taketh thy belt and weareth always for thy next touch will forever your life change. Be on your way now child.

Scene 3

Michaela
Page Patrick

Michaela walks off and is soon greeted by Page Patrick who is on a horse and returning to his manor. Michaela looks up at Patrick as he walks by.

Patrick: Peasant girl! How dare you cast your eyes on me?

Michaela: What are you talking about? You're just a kid too.

Patrick: Kid? I am not a goat you villein. I am Sir Sarcasticine's page. I shall be a knight after my training has completed. I am returning to the tournament with my lord's steed.

Michaela: (*sarcastically*) Ooooohh…you still just look like a kid in a fancy outfit to me.

Patrick: How dare you child?!? I shall strike you down. There is no need for you lousy peasants anyway.

Patrick leans off his horse to strike Mitchell with his dagger. He loses his balance and falls off.

Michaela: Wow…I see your knight lessons are really paying off.

Michaela then jumps on Patrick and they wrestle for the dagger. Suddenly, mystical music plays in the background and they change personalities. Michaela is now the page, and Patrick is the lowly peasant.

Patrick: Wait…wait…what happened? Why are you in my clothes?

Mitchell: Unbelievable! It worked. That Merlion wasn't crazy after all. Wow…I should talk to strangers more often.

Patrick: What did you say? What happened? Why am I a girl?

Michaela: Oh nothing, your highness. It just appears that you are now a lowly peasant girl and I am the page to Sir Sarcasticine.

Patrick: No one will believe you. You have no chivalry. You have no honor. They will all see right through you. I shall tell everyone about this trickery.

Michaela: Great idea. Hey…why don't you go back to my cottage and tell my brothers and sisters? They should have a great surprise for you waiting in the forest. Thanks again. Oh…and don't worry about being a peasant. You don't have to work on Sundays and you can take a swim in the river next summer for your annual bath.

Patrick: You mean…you mean…I'm going to smell as bad as you.

Michaela: I hate to break it to you page boy, but…you already smell like you've been spending too much time near the farmyard mud. I'd love to keep talking to you, but I have a tournament I need to go to.

Patrick: But…but…but…

Scene 4

Narrator #2
Michaela
Page Donald
Page Mailes
Sir Sarcasticine
Gunther

Narrator #2: Michaela hops on the horse and gallops off toward the tournament. After miles of riding, she approaches the Bloomfield Manor where tents have been set up and there is a bustling of activity. Sir Sarcasticine looks just a little frustrated.

Sir Sarcasticine: Page! Page! Where have you been? Picking daisies for your mother?

Michaela: No sir…I…uh…ran into some trouble in the forest.

Sir Sarcasticine: Well, thank you for not coming on time. Look at how much time has passed. (*Looks at hour glass*) I would have hated to have been able to prepare before my joust. Luckily now I'll be totally rushed and most likely get speared.

Michaela: Excuse me?

Sir Sarcasticine: Well, hurry up. My armor isn't going to just jump onto me.

Michaela: Yes sir.

Sir Sarcasticine: Fetch me my chain mail.

Michaela: Your what?

Sir Sarcasticine: Chain mail. You know...those annoying little letters you get from your so-called friends where they tell you you're going to get a hairy toes virus if you don't pass it on?

Michaela: Excuse me?

Sir Sarcasticine: Ahhh...my naïve little neophyte. Chain mail is the protection I put onto my chest prior to the armor.

Michaela: Right, right. I knew that.

Narrator #2: While Michaela helped Sir Sarcasticine with his helmet, pauldrons, cuisses and couleurs, another set of pages pass by practicing their dueling techniques.

Donald: On guard you wimpy little sheep herder.

Mailes: Who are you calling wimpy? You can't even throw the javelin.

Donald: Oh yeah...your momma wears leather shoes.

Mailes: Hey...all are moms wear leather shoes.

Pages continue their dueling off stage. Scene returns to Sir Sarcasticine and Michaela.

Sir Sarcasticine: Well, my boy. Thank you for your help. I can't tell you how thankful I am for you pinching my skin in the armor and banging my head with the helmet. Your hands are as gentle as a blind one-eyed giant with webbed fingers. Now, go off with your page buddies and make yourself useful.

Mailes: Patrick! Over here. Join us. I was just reminding Donald about his javelin throwing disability.

Michaela: Patrick? Uhh…my name is Micha…right…right…Patrick.

Donald: You feeling OK, Patrick?

Michaela: Yeah. I'm fine.

Mailes: Hey guys, do you want to get Gunther to practice with us?

Donald: Gunther, the oldest page in the history of the Middle Ages? That guy will never be dubbed a knight.

Mailes: Yeah. Let's get him. Even though he is a little awkward. At least when he falls down, it's fun to watch.

Donald: Oh…Gunther.

A tall, awkward-looking man, Gunther, comes on stage.

Gunther: Hey guys, are we gonna wrestle?

Mailes: Yes Gunther. But be careful this time.

Donald: OK…you pair up with Patrick. And I'll pair up with Mailes.

Narrator #2: Gunther then shows why he never has made it to a knight. He starts his sumo wrestling routine.

Gunther prepares to sumo wrestler.

Mailes: No Gunther, not Japanese wrestling.

Gunther then starts arm wrestling.

Donald: No Gunther, not arm wrestling. Don't you know what wrestling is?

Narrator #2: Then Gunther approaches Patrick and tries out a move he learned from the realm of W.W.F.

Mailes: Gunther! Stop now! Bad overgrown page! Bad page!

Donald: Now go away Gunther and let us practice.

Gunther cowers and then walks off stage.

Narrator #2: The three young pages then practiced the skills they would use many times in their knight training. They threw the javelin. They practiced acrobatics. They fought with a sword and buckler. And they practiced fighting with a quarterstaff.

Michaela: Guys, I have to leave. Here comes my master. I think he's getting ready for the joust.

Scene 5

Herald
Michaela
Page Donald
Page Mailes
Sir Sarcasticine
Sir Fearful
Lady Purity

Herald: Hearyee! Hearyee! The tournament of knights will begin in a moment. Sir Fearful has challenged Sir Sarcasticine to a joust. First, I would like to present Lady Purity.

Lady Purity enters the tournament and takes her position on the royal chair. The audience responds with "Ooohh…ahhhh".

Herald: Smellye! Smellye! Now…I would like to introduce Sir Sarcasticine. (*wait for cheering*) Now…I would like to introduce Sir Fearful (*wait for booing*) Each knight will attack their opponent at full speed on their faithful steed. They will then try to unhorse each other with their lance. They shall receive one point for a broken lance and five points for unhorsing. Are the knights ready?

Sir Fearful: Ready.

Sir Sarcasticine: No…I'm just sitting here waiting to see if my horse will turn into a camel.

Herald: At the sound of the royal bell, begin the charge.

Bell rings and two knights (on tricycles) come charging at each other. At the first pass, they both miss. They line up their tricycles and again make a charge. Crowd "Ooohs" and "Ahhhs".

Sir Sarcasticine: Wow…I can't tell you how thankful I am that this armor weights over fifty pounds…Hey, how about you and I go to my place and we settle this over a nice, hot cup of ale.

Sir Fearful: Will it have marshmallows?

Sir Sarcasticine: Well…no.

Sir Fearful: Prepare to die!

Sir Sarcasticine: Hey, knight buddy. Didn't someone tell you this was a "joust of peace". Can't we all just get along?

Michaela: Oh no! Sir Fearful is using a sharp lance instead of one with a blunt tip. If he hits Sir Sarcasticine he will surely die.

The bell rings and they charge again. This time Sir Sarcasticine dodges out of the way and hits Sir Fearful, knocking him off the tricycle.

Sir Fearful: Help! Help! I've fallen and I can't get up.

Sir Sarcasticine: Ah…it looks like your attempt to kill me has been foiled. Oh…and don't get me wrong. I was really, really scared. Really, I was. That horse of yours is pretty intimidating.

Sir Fearful: How dare you mock me? Your sarcastic comments are no match for my dagger.

Sir Fearful's page runs onstage and rolls Sir Fearful over. Sir Fearful takes the dagger and runs over to Lady Purity. The audience gasps.

Lady Purity: Oh me. Oh my. I can't believe I might soon die.

Sir Fearful: Yes, my rhyming maiden. Your life is in danger. Now I will take you away to my manor where you will be locked in my keep and all the servants will walk by and throw food at you.

Suddenly, Sir Fearful grabs Lady Purity and they run off.

Sir Fearful: If anyone tries to stop me, Lady Purity will see her twenty-five year lifespan cut in half. (*Laughs wickedly*)

Audience: Oh no…what will we do?

Michaela: (*jumps down from audience*) This is a job for Mighty Michaela!!!

Donald and Mailes: Who?

Michaela: Oh…I mean…uh…Page Patrick. This is a job for Page Patrick. I shall go save Lady Purity! (*She whistles for her horse and then jumps on*) High O Silver!

She then leaves on her trusty tricycle Silver.

Donald: Wow!!! That horse is faster than a snail being chased by an army of salt soldiers.

Scene 6

Narrator #3
Sir Fearful
Michaela
Lady Purity
Penelope the Royal Painter
Peasant #1
Peasant #2
Peasant #3
Sir Valiant

Narrator: After walking for days, Sir Fearful and Lady Purity finally reached the scariest, most dreaded manor in all of England, Burnett Manor. As Sir Fearful finally exited the forest, he looked up at his castle and...

Sir Fearful: Oh my Quetazacoatl! That has to be the scariest castle I've ever seen in my life. Now nobody is going to want to come over for a tea party. Who is to blame for this? Penelope, get in here right now!

Penelope: Yes master. How can I help you master?

Sir Fearful: When I left, this castle was pretty, pink and it looked just like the castle on the brochure for Disneyland. Now look at it. It's so dark and gloomy. I just feel like it does nothing for my karma.

Penelope: I don't know what you mean sir. When I was an apprentice for seven years, my master told me to accent with color. See, there's some yellow. There's some blue.

Sir Fearful: Oh...this is just horrible. Now people aren't going to have a chance to see my sensitive side. They'll think just because my name is Sir Fearful and my castle is all gloomy, that I'm not nice. It's just not fair....ahhh...get out of my sight.

Penelope: Yes, master. One more thing. Please don't be angry, but I took down those bright and cheery tapestries and hung a bunch of medieval armor on the walls. It looks quite menacing now if I do say so myself.

Sir Fearful: Oh nooo...Armor on the walls. A decorator's nightmare. Leave my sight.

Penelope walks off stage.

Lady Purity: Look...here comes someone to save my life. Wait a minute...that isn't the largest knight I've ever seen.

Sir Fearful: Ahhh...that's only a boy.

Michaela rode up right up to Sir Fearful.

Michaela: I have come to save the life of Lady Purity. Please hand her over before I am forced to embarrass you in front of your manor.

Sir Fearful: Embarrass me? You couldn't...

Michaela: Wait...is that your falcon flying away?

Sir Fearful: Pooksie...where's my Pooksie? (*Sir Fearful runs around looking for falcon*) Where? Where?

Narrator #3: Just as Sir Fearful looked for his prize, hunting falcon, Michaela took the opportunity to push Sir Fearful into the river moat. He then quickly sunk and was never seen from again.

Lady Purity: Wow…you are the most courageous boy I've ever met.

Michaela: Maybe that's because I'm not a boy.

Lady Purity: What did you say?

Michaela: Oh…I said…I wish I had bought a toy.

Lady Purity: (*confused*) OK...uh...that makes a lot of sense.

Suddenly, peasants came out of the castle and started congratulating Michaela.

Peasants: Hip, hip, hooray!!! You saved us great page.

Peasant #1: Now we can release our true master, Sir Valiant.

Peasant #2: Sir Valiant has been trapped in the dungeon for over thirty years and we've been living under the control of Sir Fearful.

Peasant #3: Look, here comes Sir Valiant now.

Sir Valiant: Thank you Page Patrick for freeing us from the wicked Sir Fearful. Even though tis not a squire, thou hast earned the right to be a knight. I shalt not live much longer and thou shalt take over this castle one day as your own. Thou hast proven thy worth.

Peasant #2: Yeaaayyyy...but go take a bath first. All soon-to-be knights must bathe before being dubbed a knight

Michaela walks off to take a bath and then returns to Sir Valiant.

Peasant #3: Come back. It's time to be dubbed.

Sir Valiant: Now, kneel down before me child. Repeat after me, I promise…

Michaela: I promise

Sir Valiant: To be obedient and loyal

Michaela: To be obedient and loyal

Sir Valiant: To the Burnett Manor and all its inhabitants.

Michaela: To the Burnett Manor and all its inhabitants.

Sir Valiant: I now pronounce you lord and knight. You may kiss your sword.

Everyone applauds and they all walk off stage congratulating Sir Michaela.

Scene 7

Narrator #4
Narrator #5
Narrator #6
Michaela
Sir Donald
Sir Mailes
Gunther

Narrator #4: Twenty years had passed since Michaela became Sir Patrick, lord of Burnett Manor. In that time, the manor had flourished. The harvests were full of peas, cabbage, onions and garlic. Pigs and chickens could be seen all over the land being herded by their shepherds.

Narrator #5: Sir Michaela had gotten rid of the law of the demesne, where the peasants had to work on the lord's land. Instead, Michaela herself worked on the land right alongside the peasants and she ordered all the clergy to work also.

Narrator #6: At first they saw this as too great a change from the feudal system where peasants, nobles and clergy never worked together and were separated by divisions. However, over time, they grew fond of Michaela and their new freedoms. These freedoms and peace would soon change with the coming of war.

Sir Donald: But Sir, I am afraid.

Michaela: Fear is natural. To be fearful is to be alive. To run from your fears is shameful. To face them is the honorable choice for any knight.

Sir Donald: Wow...that was really deep.

Michaela: Thank you. I read it once in Chicken Soup for the Middle Ages.

Sir Mailes: But have you heard of what happens during the Crusades? There is a chance we all might perish. Where will we get food? How can we fight the Muslims? They are stronger fighters than we could ever imagine.

Sir Michaela: Sir Mailes, I understand your fear, but it is our obligation. We all swore an oath to defend Burnett Manor. Our code of chivalry demands we honor our vow. We must go. Gunther!!!

Gunther: (*enters clumsily*) Yes Sir.

Sir Michaela: Prepare our horses. We are off to the lands of Palestine to recapture our Holy Land.

Scene 8

Narrator #7
Michaela
Peasant #4
Peasant #5
Patrick

Narrator #7: After two years, Sir Patrick (you know her as Michaela) returned tired and weary from the crusades. Her manor had been watched by the town elected reeve, but the entire town was excited to have their lord back.

Sir Michaela walks through town on his way back to his castle

Peasant #4: Sir Patrick, welcome home. How was your journey sire? How were the battles? Were the Muslims as bad as everyone says?

Sir Michaela: I do not wish to speak of war. The Muslims did what they thought was correct and we did what we thought was correct. I will not speak of the battles any more. I am weary from travel and only want to speak of peace and…

Suddenly a man bursts through the crowd.

Patrick: Peace you say? Peace? How can you say peace when I have lived as a peasant girl? You weren't very peaceful twenty years ago when you stole my identity.

Peasant #5: Quiet that woman! She obviously has the Black Death. She can not speak to our lord like that. He has honored his manor with his chivalrous fighting at war.

Patrick: He? He? He you say? This lord of yours is an imposter. I am the true Sir Patrick and I have waited years to reclaim my rightful place. I am not a peasant. I am Sir Patrick.

Peasant #4: Silence the woman, she must be punished for this heretic blasphemy.

Patrick: Doubt me do you? Watch what happens to your lord without her belt?

There is a struggle between Patrick and Michaela and when the emerge from the skirmish. Patrick is holding the belt. The entire audience shrieks in surprise.

Peasant #4: He's…he's…he's…a…she!!!

Michaela: Does it matter that I am a woman? I can do the same job as a man.

Sir Patrick: Silence woman! I am lord now, and you are banished to the fate of a peasant. I have been a woman for almost twenty years and now you shall pay. Come! My castle needs preparing. I want the great hall in the keep decorated for a feast.

Peasant #5: Yes, my lord. Shall I have the royal cook prepare the four and twenty blackbirds baked in a pie?

Sir Patrick: Yes...of course. I will be eating all alone. It is almost winter time and you can all stay in the outer bailey as punishment for your stupidity. How could you let a woman become lord? Oh...and if those blackbirds begin to sing...

Narrator #7: The evil Sir Patrick then retreated to his castle where he enjoyed his feast alone while the others stayed outside. In the following year, the townspeople quickly learned to hate their new lord, the evil, vile Sir Patrick.

Scene 9

Peasant #6
Peasant #7
Peasant #8

Peasant #6: Man, I really am starting to hate my life.

Peasant #7: Yeah, do you guys ever get the feeling we're always working for other people.

Peasant #8: You're right. First we have to work on Sir Patrick's demesne. Then we work on our land.

Peasant #6: And when it's all said and done, we have to give a tithe of 10% to the church.

Peasant #7: Sometimes I sure do feel like a slave.

Peasant #8: The only difference is we at least have the freedom to starve to death in the winter if there is a bad harvest.

Peasant #6: Life sure was better with the old Sir Patrick...I mean Michaela.

Peasant #7: I'd rather have my lord be a woman than have to live like this.

Peasant #8: Lord be a woman? Wow...you are so progressive.

Peasant #6: You know, we should talk to people in the market and see what they think.

Scene 10

Narrator #8
Michaela
Peasant #9
Peasant #10
Peasant #11
Merlion
Gunther
Cyrdon Siegeman

Narrator #8: A few times a year merchants would come from all over Europe to buy and sell their goods. These trade fairs were usually on the same day as the feast days of saints—the holy days. In addition to trading goods, these fairs were also places for entertainment. If you were talk walk through a village fair, you might see musicians, acrobats or players.

Peasant #9: Hey look. Here comes Gunther, the world's oldest page. Hey Gunther what are you doing?

Gunther: Well, I wasn't a very good page. I got stuck in my helmet for three weeks and no one could get me out. Plus, I had trouble learning manners and how to be obedient. I can be a real handful sometimes.

Peasant #10: Yeah, I bet. So what are you doing here?

Gunther: I thought about becoming a Renaissance man, a man who can do it all and still have time to explore his feelings.

Peasant #11: But the Renaissance isn't for another 400 years.

Gunther: Oh…I didn't think of that. Ahhh, and I just learned all these new tricks. Look…I can juggle. I can act. I can even play music and sing. Great. That's just great. What am I ever going to do with all these useless talents now? I might as well just become a teacher or something.

Peasant #9: Sorry, but you have to be a priest to teach.

Gunther: Ahhhh…chicken! I feel so stifled with this whole feudalism thing. I feel like a prisoner chained to the bottom of the social ladder.

Merlion: Oh crabby man who dwells on things he can not change, can I interest you in some wool, some spices, some jewelry? How about some silk from the east? How about some china from China?

Gunther: China comes from China?

Michaela starts walking toward the group.

Peasant #10: Hey guys…isn't that Michaela coming this way. I can't believe she has the nerve to come into town after what happened.

Peasant #11: I actually miss her. Life sure was better when she was Lord.

Peasant #9: Yeah…we didn't have to work on the demesne for the lord. We had off Saturdays and Sundays. Not just Sundays. The lord even invited us into the keep.

Michaela: Hey trader…don't I know you?

Merlion: Well, I used to be a magician, but I kept giving away all my tricks, so I had to go find some more stuff and things. I ended up joining this guy named Marco Polo who took me all over Asia.

Peasant #11: Isn't Marco Polo that game you play in the pool?

Michaela: No, he's the great Merchant who crossed central Asia to meet Chinese merchants.

Merlion: I would have more money too if that lord didn't keep charging me such incredible taxes. He needs to be killed.

Peasant #9: Michaela, you should be our lord again.

Michaela: You know, you guys still can have all that. All we have to do is overthrow the lord.

Peasant #10: It isn't that easy. He has all the weapons.

Peasant #11: Yeah if we get caught, we might be fined, thrown into prison or beheaded.

Gunther: Nope…actually you'll probably be hanged. Beheading is only for nobles. No matter. My principal always used to say, "If you can dream it, you can become it." All we need to do is find someone who can lead us. Someone who is strong. Someone who is powerful. Someone who knows how to use a crossbow, a catapult, a trebuchet, and a battering ram. Someone who can conjugate a verb. Someone who knows how to spell onomatopoeia. (*Entire village starts walking toward Gunther as he delivers his speech*) Someone who doesn't mind eating the same lentil soup every single day. We all know who that man is. We need….we need….we need… Cyrdon Siegeman.

Entire Village: Cyrdon Siegeman!?!?

Just then Cyrdon Siegeman comes walking into the fair.

Cyrdon Siegeman: I have been summoned. What do you need from me? Hurry up villagers. I am making my pilgrimage to the great cathedral in Spain. I have little time for these silly little jaunts. Do you think I just wander the land in this flamboyant dress looking for adventure?

Michaela: Well...yes.

Cyrdon: You're right...but what is it you need from the great Cyrdon Siegeman?

Michaela: Cyrdon Siegeman, can you save us? My villagers want me to retake Burnett Manor, but we can not do it without your help. Will you help us?

Cyrdon Siegeman: What can you give me if I do this for you?

Michaela: We have nothing. Haven't you heard? We are peasants. Everything we have we give to our lord. Even when we die we still have to pay taxes on our death.

Cyrdon Siegeman: Fine then, my pathetic little rubble. Here is what I want. I want this manor to be renamed Cyrdon Manor. I want my name plastered on a ton of cereal boxes. I want a fairy tale written about me where I get to save a beautiful princess. I want—

Michaela: Fine, fine. Whatever. What do we do?

Cyrdon Siegeman: Now, betwixt the night of the third moon doth coupleth the start thy fearful lord shalt be besieged doeth come with thy terror...

Michaela: Ummm… Cyrdon Siegeman…could you not speak in Old English, we really have no idea what you are saying.

Entire village shakes their heads and shrugs their shoulders.

Cyrdon Siegeman: We have work to do, let us prepare.

Scene 11

Narrator #9
Narrator #10
Cyrdon Siegeman
Tunneler
Gunther
Trebucheters
Battering Rammers
Lady Michaela
Sir Patrick
Damsels in Distress
Vanna

While narrators are describing castle, Vanna is demonstrating the purpose of each item.

Narrator #9: Cyrdon Siegeman took a few weeks to ready the villagers for their attack on the castle. The castle would be difficult to capture. It had rocky ledges which would be impossible to climb. It had walls of stone three feet thick.

Narrator #10: It had murder holes where men would drop fire, rocks and dead animals. If you tried to climb the walls, men stood over the machicolations to drop more rocks, or burning water, or spikes. And…the whole time…soldiers would be shooting arrows at you.

War music begins playing in the background.

Cyrdon Siegeman: Take your positions. The attack of the castle will begin shortly. Tunneler begin your tunneling. Once you're under the walls start picking away at the castle's foundation.

Tunneler: Yes sir!

Cyrdon Siegeman: Gunther…help everyone with their weapons.

Gunther: Yes sir!

Cyrdon Siegeman: Damsels in distress! Go over yonder and begin distressing.

Cyrdon Siegeman: Trebucheters. Begin trebucheting!

Trebucheters: Shall we use the heads of prisoners for ammunition.

Cyrdon Siegeman: No…that is a little bit too gross. This is family entertainment. Use the dreaded stuffed animals.

Trebucheters: Yes sir.

Trebucheters begin firing stuffed animals over the castle.

Cyrdon Siegeman: Battering rammers! Begin the battering. We need to knock that barbican down and lower the bridge.

Battering rammers: Yes sir!

Battering rammer gets hit by an arrow that comes out of arrow loop hole.

Cyrdon Siegeman: Oh…and watch out for the arrows from the arrow loop hole.

Battering rammer: Thank you sir. A little too late sir.

Cyrdon Siegeman: Spearers, begin throwing your spears, and watch out for those arrows.

Sir Patrick: You will not defeat me. I am king of this castle. I can not be defeated.

Cyrdon Siegeman: Umm...you're not a king. You're simply a lord. And yes...you will be defeated.

Tunneler: Gunther, Gunther. Get in here now. I broke through.

Gunther quickly rushes into the tunnel and into the castle. The barbican opens and the drawbridge is let down.

Gunther: Yeahh...I did something good. I did something good. I did something good. I did something....(*starts singing*) Looks like I made it (*Barry Manilowesque*)

Suddenly he is stabbed from behind and falls to the ground. Cyrdon Siegeman and his troops storm the castle and then carry Sir Patrick out the gates.

Sir Patrick: You won't have Tricky Sir Patrick to kick around anymore. (*Sir Patrick holds up his hands in a peace sign and waves them back and forth*)

Cyrdon Siegeman: Lady Michaela, I believe the castle is yours.

The crowd cheers and Lady Michaela assumes her position on the royal throne. The entire village bows in a circle around her as she stands proud.

Lady Michaela: Let it be known. From this day forward. All men are created equal. Women are just as important as men. I will share everything I have. There will be no more barbaric punishments. The Dark Ages are over.

Villagers: Hip, Hip Hooray. Hip, Hip Hooray. Long live the queen.

Narrator: And that ladies and gentlemen is how the Middle Ages came to an end. Well…kinda.

Writing Activities for Students

Mr. Burnett's Class

WRITING IN THE CLASSROOM

Students need to learn essentially two styles of writing—fiction and expository. They'll love writing because of the first and they'll get through college with the second.

Fiction is basically story-telling. Can a student write a story others want to read? Are the characters unique and can the reader relate to them? What is the problem the character faces and does the reader really care how it is solved? Is the setting another key component in leading the character along his journey, or does the story take place in a void? Quality fiction is engaging. It becomes the task of the author to use carefully chosen words to transfer the pictures in his imagination to the mind of the reader.

Expository writing lacks the pizzazz and entertainment value of fiction, but it is arguably far more important. An organized writer is an organized thinker. A focused writer walks the reader through his reasoning. With enough proof, any opinion is valid. I can convince you the sky is red if I remind you of sunrises, sunsets, and that lovely veil of pollution that welcomes me on my commute. Conversely, I can also leave you thinking I have no true reason for my opinions if I fail to substantiate my claims.

Students can produce quality work in both areas as early as third grade. They should be expected to write engagingly in both genres. Their minds are ready. They've watched enough movies to know a good story and they've argued with their parents enough to know how to get their way. They have imaginations, they have opinions, and they are not yet so petrified of conventions and mechanical errors that they are afraid to take risks.

Before I can even start teaching writing, I first assess the students on what they can produce unassisted. Granted, the writing process includes peer editing, revisions, and publication, but I want to know what the kid can really write.

Therefore, at the beginning of the year, the students give me two timed writing samples. The first is expository. The students have a choice of two questions and they are told to write a detailed paragraph that answers the question and explains the question with reasons. Questions range from "Is school a fun place?", "Is California an enjoyable place to live?", or "What is the most interesting animal?" As the year progresses, the questions require more depth of thought , but in the beginning it is best to find a non-threatening topic that they can draw from their own experiences, regardless of previous classroom instruction.

The second piece is a fiction piece. Around the room, pictures hang that engage the children's imagination. Based on a picture of their choice, they have ten minutes to brainstorm a story and thirty minutes to write the story. Most students will have no idea what brainstorming means, but this is not the time for instruction. This will give you a clear gauge of where each student is coming from and how he organizes his thoughts.

These pieces are scored based on a rubric that touches on a variety of writing skills from content to mechanics. One sample rubric is included (See Table B-1). Regardless of the rubric format used, it is important to list multiple skills. Too many teachers overly focus on mechanical errors and they fail to develop the true writing ability of the child. In a rubric of over twenty skills, spelling only is listed once. As the students use and see these rubrics throughout the year, they realize spelling is a key component of writing, but it is not the only one. Ask any child on the first day of school what makes a good writer, and they'll probably say "A good speller." Overly fixating on spelling often leads to basic word choice and delayed expression of thoughts.

This is definitely not to say that mechanics have no place in writing. Whole language instruction received a negative rap because some teachers took whole language to mean that if kids just keep reading, eventually through some magical osmosis-like scenario, knowledge would enter their heads. Not true. Students need to be taught the skills both independently and then shown how to incorporate them into their daily work.

To do this, I usually break my nine-week quarters into two parts. The first six weeks, my students spend their reading/language arts (RLA) time rotating through reading and writing group instruction. Here they learn skills taught both independently and through literature. The last three weeks of the quarter, students complete the entire writing process on a social studies topic.

For the first six weeks, the students are broken into three groups that rotate to "Independent", "Reading", and "Writing". These heterogeneous groups stay together at each station for thirty minutes.

Usually, one new skill is covered a week in the writing groups. These skills are assessed throughout the year using a writing rubric (see Table B-1). Not only are the students shown the elements and skills used in fiction, they are introduced to the concept of the "Perfect Paragraph" (see Table A-1) After being introduced on Monday to the skill of the week, the class looks for the skill throughout the week in their reading groups (in addition to other story elements) and then they practice in small groups the remaining days.

In addition, once a week students incorporate their spelling words with the new writing skill. For homework, they use their spelling words that contain one or more of the writing skills taught. For example, if the skill of the week is adverbs, all spelling sentences must also include an adverb. If we are working on conjunctions, I want to see conjunctions in all their spelling sentences. These are easy to grade and you can immediately give feedback to students. Plus, the children begin thinking about how to integrate skills into their own writing.

Back in the classroom, while one of the groups is working with writing, the others are working independently or involved in the reading group. Independent work would include capitalization/punctuation review or other mechanics skills students can learn and practice on their own.

Ideally, the reading group would be supervised/instructed by another adult. However, this is not always possible. In a situation where an additional adult is not available, students can read independently, in paired groups, under the leadership of one of the more mature students, or they can work on curriculum from another subject area. Depending on the number of students and behavior issues in a class, the number of groups and stations might need to be modified. This format has worked well in classes ranging from 35 to 22 students in grades three through eight.

The last three weeks of the quarter is the time where students incorporate all the skills into one writing piece. In the weeks preceding this final piece, the students writing takes on a variety of forms (see Table A-2) However, only once a quarter do I have them go through the entire process. Usually, this final piece is related to a social studies theme or a high interest topic.

For example, for one quarter our theme was the Middle Ages. First, the students looked through Middle Age books searching for potential conflicts. The entire year we discussed the importance of a quality plot and how all quality plots revolve around conflict and resolution. The most painful stories for a teacher to read are those where the central conflict resembles something like "The boy didn't know what to eat so he…went to the store and bought some cereal. The End." Not exactly high quality literature.

Therefore we spend a few days finding potential plots. In groups, students scanned the pictures and information in books looking for anything that might turn into a conflict. They then brainstormed plots from familiar books/movies that might be adapted to fit into the Middle Ages. We then assembled a master list of conflicts that numbered into the hundreds.

For the next step, the students spend a day looking at which conflict will hold their interest for weeks. If they don't want to write about it, don't pick it. Once they've chosen their conflict, they then complete the Idea Organization sheet (see Table A-3) This sheet includes all the major story elements which will later be incorporated in a story map.

The story map phase allows the students to sketch out their ideas and also illustrations of how their story will evolve (see Tables B-2 and B-3). Usually two or three lessons are spent working with the story map. In all lessons for this three-week unit, the teacher models exactly what it will look like. Essentially, the teacher also will have a Middle Age story at the end of the unit. One of the greatest teacher techniques is modeling. Ideally, students can actually watch as you verbally walk through your thought process in preparing your ideas and transferring them to paper. While completing the story map, the students use Story Map Topics sheet to ensure they have included all main components of a quality story (see Table A-4).

These initial steps usually take the first week, but they are critical in organizing the students' thoughts. If you take time at this phase, you save a ton of time later on. An added bonus is that by the end of the first week, the students are so tired of planning their stories that they beg you to begin the rough draft process.

During the second week, students write their rough drafts. Each day is spent completing one phase of the story map. Before having the students write, it is important to give a couple mini-lessons to review skills such as dialogue, paragraph format, or figurative language. Then the children write. If they have been properly prepared throughout the quarter during the mini-lesson phase and the pre-writing phase went well, few students should need assistance at this point. This allows the teacher to circulate to help those students who struggle in putting their thoughts to paper.

Each night the students revisit their work and edit for errors. Now, for many students when they see "Editing" as homework, they assume that no homework is actually assigned. They must be held accountable for the editing phase and must show changes are made. Students must show all their changes with another color pen. In addition, students write down the first word of every sentence. They will see quite quickly if their sentences follow a monotonous, redundant pattern. At this point, they should then revisit their work and include transitional phrases, prepositional phrases or other varied openings (see Tables A-5 and A-6). Because these sentence opening skills were taught earlier in the year, these types of phrases should be usable at this stage.

When the students return the next day, it is important to hold them accountable for their night's editing. I usually employ the "Hidden Policeman" philosophy of grading where I only grade enough so that the students have no idea when I'm actually looking at everything. They are always on guard (or so I think). Also, in the younger grades, my classes employed a money system where I would fine the students for each error they did not find. Usually, I only checked their editing after the first day and maybe one other time. Depending on your classroom environment, this should be enough.

In the subsequent days, the students continue the process of writing and editing their work after a brief mini-lesson that revisits an element of strong story writing. Once completed, the students then share their work with their peers. Initially, I'll have one peer read another's piece out loud. Reading out loud is key. This way both the writer and the reader can recognize flaws. This type of reading usually uncovers a great many errors or missing plot elements. At the next phase of peer editing, the students read each other's work following the Peer Editing sheet (see Table A-7).

After the initial peer editing I hold the editor responsible for finding errors. It is a paid position. Using Burnett Bucks, students actually pay these editors to find mistakes. Any mistake not found is also a monetary fine based on my class money system. It is in the student's best interest to search for every error. Sometimes this leads to the students being hypercritical, which you will then need to discuss with them. However, I'd much prefer the hypercritical editor to the one that fails to take their role seriously.

Finally, after a week of pre-writing, a week of completing the rough draft, and a few days of peer editing, the students are prepared to write their final draft. You'll find that one noticeably absent part of this process is my hand in the editing. I truly want the work to be the student's work. The student story samples included later in this book are printed exactly as they appeared in their final draft. This is the only way I've found that I can truly teach children to have pride in their work. Once they've completed the final draft I have them share their work with peers, other teachers, and older students. Students become embarrassed to have any errors in their writing. I'd much rather have pride be the motivating factor in editing their work than the pursuit of the almighty letter grade.

Subsequently, when you read the students' stories you might find an error or two, or awkward phrasing. However, this is how the eight and nine year olds write. This philosophy is not shared by all teachers, but I'd much rather have parents see what the child actually writes than what I can write (which also usually has a few errors). The first six weeks of the quarter the students' work is edited heavily, but by this phase I want to see where they stand without adult assistance.

At the end of the year, after writing three of these pieces and completing numerous smaller writing assignments throughout the year, I assess the students again on their ability to write both an expository and fiction piece. Again, the writing rubrics are used and the students are able to visibly see their growth. To help illustrate the growth of third graders, included are two pieces that show an average student's growth from the beginning to the end of the year (See Table B-4). Even though errors still exist, this student learned to use her voice to share her opinions in an organized fashion.

By no means is this an all-encompassing presentation of how to teach writing. Like any other teaching tool, the ideas and resources presented here should be taken and modified to fit your own teaching style and the demands of your school. However, I've found that whether teaching public or private, eighth grade or third grade, the basic philosophy and skill lessons used are applicable in most environments. Best of luck and hopefully you can utilize some of the information presented.

WRITING RESOURCES

The Perfect Paragraph

A perfect paragraph **must** have the following:
1) Topic Sentence—what is the entire paragraph about?
2) Reason #1
3) Reason #2
4) Reason #3
5) Conclusion—remind reader of your three main reasons

To organize your thoughts, you can use the following transitional phrases:

Basic	Other Transitions			Conclusions
First, Second, Third,	Furthermore Moreover, In addition, Besides that, Also,			In summary, To summarize, In conclusion, To conclude, Finally,

Friends are very important. First, whenever you are depressed, friends can offer support. Second, if you are bored, a friend can play sports with you. Third, if you are confused about schoolwork, a friend can lend you a helping hand. In summary, friends are wonderful because they offer support, play sports with you, and help you out.

The Super Perfect Paragraph

Once you have mastered "The Perfect Paragraph", you can add more description by:
1) Giving an **EXAMPLE** for each reason

Friends are very important. First, whenever you are depressed, friends can offer support. If you happen to be crying, a friend can cheer you up by acting silly. Second, if you are bored, a friend can play sports with you. Instead of staring at the T.V. all day, you could grab a ball and go play basketball. Third, if you are confused about schoolwork, a friend can lend you a helping hand. Sometimes math can be confusing, but a friend can explain to you a different way of figuring out a problem. In summary, friends are wonderful because they offer support, play sports with you, and help you out.

Usually, For instance, Specifically, To illustrate,	For example, Frequently, In particular, Occasionally,

A-1

Creative Topics for Responding to Literature

I   Comic Book

II   Diary Entries of Character

III   Glossary of Story Elements

IV   Letter to a Character, Author

V   Rewrite Chapter/Ending

VI   Character Interview

VII   Newscast Describing Plot Event

VIII   Rewrite Story Elements with Song Lyrics/Poem

IX   Character Biography

X   Compare/Contrast Book with Movie

XI   Write Sequel to Book

XII   Travel Brochure

XIII   Timeline

Middle Age Fairy Tale
Idea Organization

Main Problem:

Main Solution Solved at Very End:

Who are my main characters?

Describe what your character looks like?

Describe how your character acts?

What does the world look like where the story takes place?

What are some problems that happen to your character BEFORE he can solve the problem?

1 Mini-Problem along the way:

1 Mini-Solution along the way:

2 Mini-Problem along the way:

2 Mini-Solution along the way:

A-3

Story Map Topics
Does Your Story Map Have the Following?

Setting

- Season?
- Time of Day?
- Smells?
- Sounds?
- What does land around look like?
- Any buildings around?

Character

- Age
- Skin/Hair/Eye Color
- Any scars, marks from past
- Clothes/shoes
- Jewelry
- Holding anything in hand
- What did he do to make him a good character?

Story Problem

- Who was involved—good guy and bad guy
- What happened before? How did this problem come about?
- Why is this problem bad? What could happen if the bad side wins?

Main Event #1

- What is new setting?
- How much time has passed?
- How did character get to new setting?
- Who is involved?
- What happened? What was the mini-problem?
- How did the main character solve the mini-problem?

Main Event #2

- What is new setting?
- How much time has passed?
- How did character get to new setting?
- Who is involved?
- What happened? What was the mini-problem?
- I Iow did the main character solve the mini-problem?

Story Problem Solution

- What is new setting?
- How much time has passed?
- How did character get to new setting?
- What important action happens?
- What happens to bad character?
- Now that good character won, what next?

Transitional Phrases

Changes Over Time	Supporting Details
Afterward,	Also,
By that time,	Besides that,
Earlier	For example,
First,	For instance,
From then on,	For that matter,
Later,	Frequently,
Meanwhile,	Furthermore,
Next,	Generally,
Presently,	In addition,
Soon,	In fact,
Then	In general,
	In order to _____,
	In other words,
Cause and Effect	Moreover,
As a consequence,	Occasionally,
As a result,	Similarly,
Consequently,	Specifically,
Due to _____,	Usually,
Finally,	
For this reason,	
Subsequently,	**Conclusions**
Therefore,	Finally,
	In conclusion,
	On the whole,
Comparing Like Items	To conclude,
At the same time,	To summarize,
Compared to _____	
Likewise,	
Once more,	**Comparing Different Items**
Similarly,	Even so,
	However,
	In contrast,
	Instead,
	Nevertheless,
	On the other hand,
	Unlike _____,

A-5

Prepositions

Prepositions give us more information about where and when an event is taking place.

<u>Around the corner</u> I met a group of my friends.

The two teams decided to meet at the store <u>around the corner</u>.

While I was going <u>around the corner</u>, I saw my best friend Michael.

1. above the	1. in
2. across the	2. in addition to
3. after the	3. in back of
4. against the	4. in case of
5. along the	5. in front of
6. among	6. inside
7. around	7. instead of
8. at	8. into
9. before	9. like
10. behind	10. near
11. below	11. next
12. beneath	12. of
13. beside	13. on top of
14. between	14. since
15. beyond	15. through
16. down	16. throughout
17. during	17. till
18. except	18. under
19. except for	19. underneath
20. for	20. until
21.from	41.upon

A-6

Peer Editing

Name of editor: _____

Name of author: _____

Put a check next to the following topic once you have checked for that in the paper:

☐ I   Spelling: I circled all words that might have spelling mistakes

☐ II   Verb agreement: I checked that all verbs are past tense and match the noun. I circled any mistakes.

☐ III   Run-on Sentences: For sentences that go on and on, I put in a period and capitalized the next word.

☐ IV   Fragment Sentences: I underlined all groups of words that aren't complete sentences.

☐ V   Figurative language: I put a BOX around all figurative language examples. The author I read had _____ examples.

☐ VI   Dialogue: I circled all places where the author didn't use the correct punctuation, indentation or capitalization for dialogue.

Name: Date:

Writing Rubric

Skill Knowledge:	Absent	Beginning	Mastery
Content			
Story			
Title			
Plot - Intro, Problem, Solution			
Character Personal/Physical			
Setting Time/Place			
Vocabulary			
Figurative Language			
Voice			
Graceful Ending			
Expository			
Topic Sentence			
Supporting Details			
Logical Sequence			
Conclusion			
Transitional Phrases			
Vocabulary			
Voice			

# of Errors	Numerous	Few	None
Mechanics			
Capitalization			
End Punctuation			
Internal Punctuation			
Spelling			
Subject/Verb Agreement			
Paragraph Structure			
Dialogue			
Run-Ons			
Fragments			
Ommitted Words			
Variety of Sentence Openings			
Compound Sentences			

B-1

STORY MAP

Sequence box

Setting:- When, Where. Draw the main setting in the box. Describe it in words below.

Simile:

Main Character:- Draw the main character, then describe the character in words below. Be specific.

Simile:

Main Event/Scene:- Draw one of the main scenes in your story. Tell what is happening. Give details.

Simile:

Main Event/Scene:- Draw another main scene. Write about the scene below.

Simile:

Story Problem:- Draw a picture of the problem. Explain it in words below.

Simile:

Story Problem Solution: Draw a picture of the problem being solved. Explain below how the problem gets solved.

Simile:

B-2

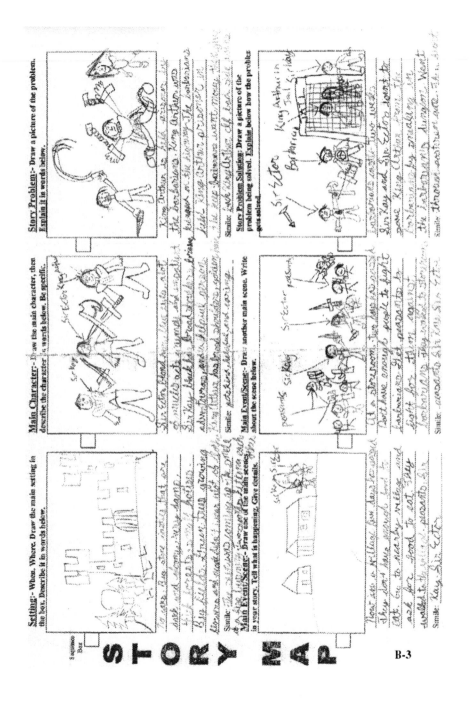

Expository – 30 mins.

Final Paragraph

STUDENT FAIRY TALES

The Stolen Jewels
Liz Quick

"Hearye! Hearye! You are invited to the King's feast," yelled the herald. Page Patrick immediately ran to his father and told him the news.

"Can we go?" said Patrick eagerly.

"Okay," said his dad with a smile.

"We will always go to any feast in the whole entire land."

Patrick was a page in training. He was nice and had dark brown hair. He was fourteen years old. Patrick could not wait to go to the feast. It was six days before the feast and it was time to leave for Camelot.

"Moey, fetch our horses! We are off to Camelot!" commanded Patrick's dad.

They rode for days and nights. Then finally, they saw Camelot in the distance. Camelot had stone cottages and each had a garden of trees and flowers. The castle stood on a hill that was as big as a giant's belly. As they rode up to the castle, the breeze blew in Patrick's face. As they got closer to the feast, they could hear music being played from the Great Hall. They tied up their horses to a post and entered the feast.

"Hearye! Hearye! We will now serve chicken!" yelled the herald. Patrick stared at his trencher as he waited for his chicken. When he looked up he saw jugglers. Something didn't look right. Where was the juggler with the black and white stripes? A scream interrupted his thoughts.

"Ah...Where are my jewels?" yelled the king.

"What?" the crowd gasped.

Just as Patrick looked in front of him, he saw the black and white juggler.

"Hmm...that's strange," mumbled Patrick.

After a while the herald announced, "Hearye! Hearye! The king wants all pages to try to find the jewels. Whoever finds the jewels will be knighted. Good luck!"

Patrick got up and started to walk toward the storeroom. There were barrels everywhere. As he trotted over to the first barrel to see what was inside, he heard a sound that sounded like juggler's bells.

"That's strange," he mumbled. As he lifted the lid of the barrel, something caught his eye. A barrel that didn't look like the other ones. It had brown stripes instead of black. He walked over to se what was inside it.

Suddenly, he fell into a trap!

"Ahhoooooo!" screamed Patrick.

"He, he" snickered the black and white juggler as he put the trap door on the trap.

"Now what am I going to do?" said Patrick.

Then something caught his eye. It was smooth and gray. It was a rock.

"Yes!" Patrick said.

He picked up a rock and threw it at the trap door. Slowly it inched open. He climbed out and headed back to the feast.

Three turns of the hourglass later, Patrick asked his dad if he could explore the castle one more time before they left. Patrick got up and headed over to the gatehouse. He opened up the door to the gatehouse. He heard people talking.

"I stole the king's jewels master. Now may I keep them?" asked the black and white juggler.

"Of course, you stupid juggler. You stole them, didn't you?" said a musician. At that moment, Patrick jumped out and pointed his sword at the juggler's throat.

"Do you yield?" asked Patrick.

"No, I don't!" yelled the juggler.

"Clash!" went their swords as they came together.

"Kkkaaaaabbbbbllllllaaaaammmmmmmm!" went Patrick's sword as it hit the juggler's chest.

"I yield!" yelled the juggler in pain.

"I will bring you back to the king and he will do what he wants to you," said Patrick.

Patrick and the juggler started to walk back to the Great Hall. Patrick entered the feast and headed over to the king.

"Sir, I found out who stole the jewels. It was this juggler," said Patrick.

"Well it looks like we found ourselves a winner," said the King. "Follow me. It's time to be dubbed."

The king led Patrick to his room and took out a sword.

"Repeat after me," said the king. "I promise to be obedient and loyal…"

Patrick repeated what the king just said and smiled. He was now a knight. He walked over to his dad and said, "Can we go now?"

"Okay," said his dad.

They rode back to their manor and told the good news. Patrick was now a knight.

Runaway
By Laura Long

Once upon a time, there lived a king, a queen and a princess named Lucy. She lived in a castle on rolling green hills with a cozy village below. The sun was going down. Lucy was nine years old, and she had every toy that was ever made. She had no friends. Her eyes were as blue as the sea, and she wore fine silk and velvet. Her long black hair almost touched the ground.

One day she asked her father for a hobby horse.

"You already have ten of those!"

"But I want eleven of them!"

"No!"

"You won't buy me anything!" Lucy yelled and ran out of the room, down the stairs and through the village and down the path to the dark, spooky forest. Later at the castle, everybody was looking for Lucy, but nobody could find her.

Meanwhile, in the dark forest, Lucy was lost, and the clouds were as dark as the bottom of the ocean. It was going to rain. Lucy tried to find a place to go in before it started to rain, but she was too late. It was raining so hard it hurt her head. Then she finally found a tree with a hole in it. She scurried and crawled into the tree for the night.

When it stopped raining, she crawled out of the tree, but it was pitch black, and she could not see a thing. There were a lot of weird and scary sounds in the forest. There were glowing eyes all looking at her. She wished she was in her nice, cozy bed. She tried to find the hole in the tree, but it was gone. She fell to the ground and cried the whole night. Then four hours later the sun began to rise. She looked around and saw all these animals looking at her. All the eyes were just animals. It was still a little dark, but it was light enough to see. So, she walked along the dirt path.

After walking for a couple of hours, she got tired and very bored. She wished she had one of her hobby horses. She was so homesick. She decided to go back home and see what everybody else was doing, but she didn't know which way was home. Then, all of a sudden, a little fairy came down and said, "I am your fairy godmother, and I am here to grant you a wish."

"A wish!" Lucy said.

"Yes."

"OK! I wish to see my family."

Then the fairy got out a crystal ball and waved her hand above it. Then her family appeared in the crystal ball.

"You can keep the crystal ball."

"Really?"

"Yes."

"Thanks!" And then the fairy flew away. She was so happy she got to see her family one more time.

After walking for a few hours, Lucy found a river. She decided to get a drink and rest. The water was so clean, cold, and refreshing. She laid back on the grass and thought about all her toys and her parents. She missed them. Meanwhile, at the castle they decided to look in the forest for Lucy.

"Ronald, get my horse!" the king said. Ronald got his horse, and he rode to the forest. Lucy was fast asleep when she heard a ruckus. She got up, and she saw a huge horse standing in front of her. Then she saw a familiar person. It was her father. She was so happy.

"Lucy, come back to the castle!" he said.

"OK, Father!" Lucy said. So Lucy and her father hopped on the horse and rode off to their castle. And later that week, they had a party celebrating the return of Lucy. And Lucy learned that her family was far more important than toys and jewels.

The Magic Armor
Gavriel Roda

Once upon a time in the town of Camelot, a tall castle stood proudly among all the tiny huts. Birds chirped and chickens screamed. The sun was getting out of bed. The grass shone from the morning dew.

A brave, kind knight with blue eyes, blond hair, and broad shoulders, Sir Dane, always rode along with his best friend, Sir Ding Dong. He was a silly lad with a skinny body, brown eyes and brown hair. Both were twenty-three years old and loved to fight. Once they slayed a fire-breathing dragon!

At that moment, Sir Dane was in the middle of a joust.

"Do you yield?" asked Sir Dane.

"I—I—I yield," said the other knight afraid Sir Dane might kill him.

"Yaaaaaaaaah, he won, he won. Woohooo!" The crowd went wild.

After winning the joust he rode home on his divine, brown stallion feeling very proud.

Suddenly, a wizard disguised as a knight rode on fast as an arrow towards Sir Dane. The wizard's lance was pointing straight at Sir Dane.

What would Sir Dane do? He couldn't fight. His sword, lance, bows and arrows were in the storage room!

"Aaaaaah!" screamed Sir Dane. Before he could move his horse out of the way, he was hit by a magic lance.

A day later he woke in his bed.

"W—w—where am I?" Sir Dane whispered. His manor was neat and tidy and his armor slept still in the corner. But why was his armor glowing? He decided to wear it anyway and go to Sir Ding Dong's manor to ask if he wanted to go out into the forest and hunt. Sir Dane felt better already.

When he arrived at the manor, Sir Ding Dong was already waiting for him.

"Ready?" asked Sir Ding Dong excitedly.

"No, not yet," said Sir Dane.

"Hey Dane, why is your armor glowing?" asked Sir Ding Dong confused.

"Nothing, um….oh…nothing. That's nothing," replied Sir Dane shyly.

"Well then, let's go!"

"No! I am not going with a dumb-dumb like you," said Sir Dane in a robot voice.

"What did you call me?!"

"A dumb-dumb, you pathetic knight!"

"How dare you call me pathetic!" hollered Sir Ding Dong.

"Too bad. I just did!" mocked Sir Dane.

"Fine, tomorrow we'll ride into the woods and see who can survive!" replied Sir Ding Dong.

"You're on!" said Sir Dane with a wicked tongue.

Deep in the heart of the green, misty woods was the vile wizard's cottage.

"I've got him now!" screeched the wizard.

"Now that I've got Sir Dane hypnotized I can take over his manor and nobody is going to stop me! Haaaa! Haaa! Haaa!!!!" The wizard made a spooky grin.

The following day Sir Ding Dong and Sir Dane were ready to go into the green mist of trees.

"Prepare to die you blubber face!" yelled Sir Dane.

"You're obviously not thinking correctly. You're the blubber face!" screamed Sir Ding Dong. As they kept on insulting each other the wizard looked at his crystal ball and smiled wickedly.

"This is perfect. Just perfect. Two of the best friends and knights just broke up. What a surprise!" cackled the wizard.

At the edge of the scary woods, the two knights were still trading insults.

"Come on, you said you wanted to see who would survive in the woods, you pig face!" babbled Sir Dane.

"Fine then. On your marks, get set, Go!" yelled Sir Ding Dong. They raced and raced, deeper and deeper into the forest.

All of a sudden, a noise of one hundred galloping horses was coming toward Sir Dane and Sir Ding Dong.

"Have no fear. Sir Dane is here. I—"

"What do you mean you're here. You're the one who's going to die!" corrected Sir Ding Dong.

"Cut it out!" yelled Sir Dane, "Or else we'll both get run over!" They ran for their lives. Sir Ding Dong climbed up a tree as Sir Dane was being chased to the end of a cliff.

"Heeeeeellllllppppp!!!" screeched Sir Dane. From out of the tree, Sir Ding Dong caught Sir Dane's armor.

"Hold on tight. I'm pulling you onto the tree!" yelled Sir Ding Dong.

At the wizard's cottage the wizard stomped his feet and screamed, "Why? Why did Sir Ding Dong help Sir Dane?"

The wizard decided to go out and make Sir Dane kill Sir Ding Dong for his stupidity in helping Sir Dane.

The wizard dressed as a knight, grabbed his lance, got on his horse and rode off into the woods. Finally, the wizard heard the two knights talking. The wizard hid behind a tree and started controlling Sir Dane to kill Sir Ding Dong. Sir Dane felt his armor take control of his body.

"Aaaaaaaaaeeeehhhh, my armor's controlling me to do something!"

Quickly Sir Ding Dong looked around for some miracle. When he saw the evil wizard controlling Sir Dane with magic, he screamed, "So you're the one who's been controlling Sir Dane's brain and armor!"

"Yes, so you finally used your brain!" insulted the mean old wizard."

"You better stop it or I'll break your only weapon—your magic lance!" said Sir Ding Dong bravely.

"I'm going to kill you!" hollered Sir Dane as he charged towards Sir Ding Dong, raising his arms above his head and swung the sword down hard towards Sir Ding Dong.

Sir Ding Dong ducked and grabbed the lance from the wizard's cold hands.

"Three, two, one!" counted Sir Ding Dong ready to break the lance in half.

"Zero!" and with that, he broke the lance in half.

Fireworks, glitter, pink smoke and fire sprung out like a rocket from the lance while the wizard turned into a black puff of smoke and disappeared.

There was silence for a minute and Sir Dane spoke, "Huh? What happened? Why am I in the forest?"

"It's a long story. I'll tell you later." So the two friends rode home with their arms draped on each other's shoulders, and lived happily jousting ever after.

Andrew's Amazing Journey
Skye Casey

Once upon a time in a great castle in Burgundy, there lived a ten year old boy called Andrew. Andrew was actually King of Arran since his parents had been killed in an invasion. Fenella, a seventeen year old girl, hid Andrew from the barbarians. Jordan, a twenty year old man, also hid Andrew from the barbarians. Jordan was Fenella's fiance who was kind, loyal, brave and calm.

Every morning as the moon went to bed, and the sun got up, Andrew would slip on his clothes, run down the dark, cold staircase, and would sit under the big oak tree, eating a loaf of bread. He missed his parents terribly and promised himself that he would return to Arran.

Fenella was helpful, kind, loyal and determined. She had a very strong sense of right and wrong.

"Andrew, Jordan's waiting to take you riding!" Fenella called from the drawbridge.

"Coming. In a second," Andrew replied. Andrew ran to Jordan, got on his horse and rode like the wind. They then rode all around the whole town and just wanted to have a nap on top of the clouds.

At ten thirty every morning, Andrew would have a sword fighting lesson.

"If you keep this up, you'll be the best swordsman in Burgundy," Jordan announced.

"Better than Uncle Phillipe?"

"Of course!" Jordan replied.

"Better than you?"

"Of course not!"

Ever since Andrew's parents were killed he was sad and lonely. He could still remember how the terrifying sight happened. An arrow shot through his mother's back and a sword through his father's chest.

"Andrew, are you feeling all right?" Jordan asked.

"Yes, just fine," Andrew replied. Andrew remembered running. But Andrew knew he would fight back some day.

"Andrew, it's time for you to have some tea," Fenella shouted on the drawbridge. Andrew hurried to the castle.

Jordan thoughts went back to the night of his escape.

The Barbarians had come from Antoich and wanted Arran's gold. Antoich had an evil king with lips as red as blood and eyes that were black as the midnight sky. He wore a black, shagged cape and red velvet boots.

Andrew hated leaving his home, but he knew that the Barbarians would have hunted him down until they killed him. They couldn't have the new king alive. He had to run away.

Fenella and Jordan helped Andrew escape. They dressed him in one of Fenella's maid's outfits. They put dirt on his face and hands. Then Fenella tied a scarf around his head.

"You must pretend to be a servant," Fenella said. "Don't look at anyone but me and Jordan."

Andrew and Fenella climbed into a cart and hid under the straw. Jordan and another loyal soldier to Andrew's father navigated the road to the sea. From beneath the straw, Andrew saw many houses on fire. He was only ten but shaking with anger at the Barbarians.

At the sea, a Barbarian stopped them.

"Who goes there?" he shouted.

Jordan said, "I am from Burgundy and I am going home. You have no right to stop me."

"Who goes with you?" the soldier demanded to know.

"My assistant, my wife, and her serving girl. We are all from Burgundy."

"Let me see them," the soldier yelled.

Quivering like a rattle, Andrew stood up with Fenella. The soldier stared meanly at them. Suddenly the soldier lunged like a bear at them.

Andrew jumped back and the man laughed. Andrew wanted to hit him, but remembered Fenella's warning. Instead, he looked at his feet and tried not to cry.

Finally the soldier said, "You may pass."

Jordan showed them to the ship. He told Andrew that he must pretend to be a girl until they reached Burgundy.

"Andrew, tea time. Come now before it gets too cold," Fenella shouted again.

Andrew snapped back to the present.

He would find a way back to Arran. He would return. Oh yes, he would return.

Five years later, Andrew visited his uncle in Burgundy. He told Uncle Phillipe the whole story, but Andrew's uncle didn't believe him.

"How can I prove I was able to escape Arran?" Andrew thought to himself.

"Ask him if you can go to Arran and help take it back," Jordan suggested.

"Thank you so much!" Andrew cried while running to his uncle's room.

"Uncle Philippe!" I can come to Arran with you and help you take over!" Andrew cried running out of breath.

"I'm sorry, but there is no way you're going to Arran with me to help me take over. Listen, it would be wonderful if you did, but I don't want you to be killed the way your father did," he said.

"But I can prove it, ask Jordan and Fenella!" Andrew said furiously and ran out of the room.

"Andrew wait!" Uncle Philippe said getting out of his chair. "He's fifteen and is great at riding. Oh what have I done?" Uncle Philippe asked himself. As Uncle Philippe trotted down the staircase, he was calling Andrew's name but there was no answer. Where was he?

Suddenly, Uncle Phillipe heard shouting.

"Invaders! The castle is under attack!" shrieked a villager.

"Men, get your armor and take your places as quick as possible!" Uncle Philippe commanded. "Jordan, go to the north wall and stay there."

"Yes sir," Jordan said and marched off.

"Andrew...where's Andrew!?" Uncle Philippe yelled.

"I'll find him, sire, and make sure he's safe," a page promised.

Uncle Phillipe rushed off to check the west side of the castle. From the parapet, he could see a young horseman leading the charge against the invasion.

"Who's that?" he asked himself. "Oh my gosh! That's Andrew!" he yelled. He ran through the dark castle and caught up with Andrew.

"What are you doing?" Uncle Philippe asked.

"Something I should have done a long time ago," Andrew replied.

"Stop! Do you want to end up the way your parents did?"

"My parents tried to defend a little boy. I'm not a little boy anymore," Andrew said defiantly.

Andrew remembered something his mother always told him—Have faith in yourself.

"Charge!" Andrew said with pride.

"You're a brave lad, Andrew. You're a brave lad," Uncle Philippe said to himself.

"We'll win this war Uncle Philippe. I promise we will," Andrew said with determination.

"We have a strong army, all thanks to you. I'm positive Andrew," Uncle Phillipe said.

The war went on for five days and eventually Andrew's army had won.

"Andrew, I'm glad you're my nephew and am very proud of you," Uncle Phillipe said proudly.

Jordan walked toward Andrew and Uncle Phillipe and announced, "Fenella and I are getting married today since the war ended!"

"Wow! Oh my gosh. I can't believe it!" Andrew said. Fenella came running into the room.

"D...di...did you hear?" Fenella cried out of breath.

"Yes, it's wonderful and I'm sure you'll be a wonderful couple," Andrew replied.

"I'm pleased you're getting married and I know Andrew's in good hands if anything happens to me," Uncle Phillipe said.

"What could happen to you?" Andrew asked.

"Well son, we're going to Arran to take over," said Uncle Phillipe.

"I'm coming with you," said Andrew. "You know I'm ready."

The ships sailed into Arran at night. Jordan knew the way, so they weren't afraid of getting lost. The men were as quiet as mice as they got their armor on. Andrew promised himself that he would win this fight for his father and mother.

Even before the sun was in the sky, Andrew, Phillipe, and Jordan were riding to the castle. Their hearts were pounding as hard as the horse's hooves. Andrew rode to the east, Phillipe rode to the west, and Jordan rode to the north of the castle. Each had one hundred men. When Phillipe sounded the horn, they began their attack. They got into the castle before the guards knew what to do. Using his sword, Andrew fought his way to the evil king's bedroom. He found him hiding in a secret closet. Andrew remembered playing there as a child.

"Surrender to the true King of Arran!" shouted Andrew.

"Don't kill me," begged the evil king.

Andrew thought for a minute. As he did, the wicked man tried to stab him with a small dagger. Luckily, Jordan killed him with an arrow from the door.

"You saved my life, again," Andrew whispered. Then he smiled because he knew he was home at last."

Some villagers from Arran came up to Andrew, got on their hands and knees and said, "Oh, thank you my lord."

"I will help you in any way I can," Andrew promised. He was already dreaming of living in the castle again.

"Andrew, you don't have to stay with Fenella and me in Burgundy," Jordan suggested.

Andrew turned and stared at Jordan.

"I've got a better idea. You and Fenella come here when there's an invasion in Burgundy."

"If it makes you happy," Jordan replied. As Jordan finished his last word, Fenella came dashing in the room.

"Oh my word!" Fenella screamed as she looked at the dead body.

"Don't worry. I killed him," Jordan said. "Andrew's staying here and we'll help each other if there's an invasion."

"Oh, okay. I only want to make you happy."

"You sure this is all right guys?" Andrew asked.

"Sure, it's all right. Tonight I want us to have a feast for you and our wedding," Fenella said cheerfully.

Later that night they had a huge feast. Everyone in Arran came to the castle and they all lived safely and happily ever after.

Lucky
Jaime Lin

Once upon a time, during the Middle Ages, there lived a little girl called Michaela. She lived with her mother called Heidi, her father called Geardon, and a seventeen year old brother called Matt.

They all lived in a manor called Gray Manor.

Michaele was nine. She liked to go into the forest and talked to her animal friends.

It was a secret though. Nobody knew and Michaela always went alone.

Michaela had light skin, bright blue eyes that were as blue as the sky, golden hair that shined in the sunlight, wore silk clothes, and wore leather shoes.

On Michaela's ninth birthday one of her presents was a pair of magic shoes. They would grant her any wish she wanted in the whole world, but she could only have three wishes.

Michaela loved her magic shoes. The shoes were waterproof. She even wore them when she went swimming.

One day, when Michael came back from swimming she got in the house and changed, a rat carrying the Black Plaque went into Heidi's room.

Then, all of a sudden the fleas on the rat got onto Heidi.

Heidi caught the dreadful Black Plaque !!

Mother, mother, are you okay?!" Michaela asked worryingly. "What happened?!"

"I... caught the.. Black... Pla.... Pla...."

"Plack? Plate?, Play? What is it?!!"

"I caught the ... Black... Pla.. Pla... Plaque...." Heidi coughed.

"Oh Noo!!" Michaela screamed.

"Calm... down." Heidi said

"Well, how did you catch it?!"

"A rat… came… in and the ….. fleas o… on.. it got on me…."

"G RRRRRRRRRRRR!" Michaela growled angrily.

Michaela walked around. She found the rat, and kicked it out of the house.

"When Matt and Goerdon heard the noise they came running into the room.

"What happened!!" they both said franticly.

"Eaahcckkerahcckkeacckk!!!"

"Good… bye …my…loving… family. I love .. you … all obviously Matt the best but…. I love you… all ….

"Noooooooooooooooooooo!!" Matt, Goerdon, and Michaela cried.

Three days later, Heidi was buried. Matt and Goerdon also died of the Black Plaque and Michaela was all alone.   It was Sunday. The moon went to sleep and the sun just got out of bed. The grass was wet with dew and the towns people were waking up, getting ready for their day.

Michaela gathered some of her belongings, got some bread, some smoked meat, and a trencher and packed it in her little leather bag. Then she set off living on her own. When Michaela was walking out of town, a crowd of people, were chasing her.

"Let's get her!," a man said.

"Oh—no!! They're going to kill me!!"

Michaela ran away from them as fast as she could. She ran straight into a forest. She was safe.

As Michaela was walking through the forest the sun went down, and the moon got out of bed. It was very dark and the stars were shining profoundly in the sky.

An hour had passed since Michaela had run away from the townspeople.

She was very tired. She was looking for a path to get out of the forest but she couldn't. She was lost!!

"I know what to do!" I'll wait till morning to find a path. It will be easier to find one because it will be brighter to see!!" Michaela thought.

So, while Michaela waited for morning to find a path she went to a big rock, laid her things out, had some smoked meat, and went to bed.

The next morning she went around, looking for a path to get out. Finally, after searching, for three hours.

Michaela walked out of the forest on a dirt road happily.

She was saved.

A day had passed since Michaela got out of the forest.

When Michaela was walking on the dirt path, she came to a river.

The river was flowing so fast that it seemed as if the rocks in the river were flowing away.

"Oh—No!! How will I ever cross this river?! What will I do?! Michaela wondered frantically.

Michaela walked around, trying to find a way to get across the river.

Then, she got an idea. Michaela saw a few logs. She picked them up and tied them together with a vine. Then she got another vine and tied it to the raft. There was a looper at the other side of the river.

Michaela threw the vine over the loop. Then she got on the raft and pulled herself across.

"Hooray!!" Michaela said happily. "I got across the river!! Now I can go on!"

Then Michaela continued on her adventures journey.

It was dawn. Michaela had walked for hours. She finally reached the town while she was thinking that she was too young to take care of herself.

So, she went back to her manor.

While she was on her way, the townspeople came up to her and said, "You are worthless!!" Your family died of the Black Plaque and you can't even take care of yourself, so you might-as-well die!!"

Oh—No!! They're trying to kill me again! Someone please save me!! Ahhh!!"

"I will!" A boy said. "I will save you from the townspeople!:

This boy's name was Daren Heigley.

He was the same age as Michaela. He made weights to work out with, and he always helped people with frustrating things.

"Hooray!!" Michaela screamed happily. "Someone has come to save my life!"

"Don't touch her or else."

"Why should we listen to you?" a man said.

"Because if you don't, you will die." Daren threatened.

"Oh my hero!" Michaela said dreamily.

Then Daren showed why the townspeople would die.

He got a sword that was lying on the ground and cut the man's head off.

"Ok-Ok, we get the point," all the other townspeople said, and they ran away.

"Oh thank you sir. What is your name?" Michaela asked.

"Daren tis my name. Helping people tis my game."

"Oh Michaela, will you marry me?"

"Yes, Sir Daren, I will."

Two years later, Michaela had a child. A daughter called Marriane. She was beautiful, kind, gentle and very loving, and all three of them, Michaela, Daren and Marriane lived happily ever after.

The Brave Knights
Paul Ban

Once upon a time in the land of Camelot there lived a king and his knights.

One day, King Arthur set off alone on a mission to another castle. He had to go through a thick spooky forest.

King Arthur was a brave, helpful, caring person. He wore a gold velvet robe on the inside and a shining armour on the outside. There was a sword he held called Excalibur. King Arthur was a friendly person because he helped people with their problems.

Suddenly twenty barbarians jumped out from behind the bushes.

"Have your hands up or we will kill you," said one of the barbarians.

King Arthur put up his hands.

"Tie him up you dogs!" roared a barbarian.

The barbarians were as big as trees.

King Arthur was dragged to a dark and gloomy stone castle. King Arthur could see small houses and fields right next to the castle.

Outside the castle gates, King Arthur was so hot he asked some barbarians to take off his armour. King Arthur could see the sun coming up and could smell smoke. Suddenly he heard two swords clashing against each other.

When King Arthur got to the barbarian's castle he was thrown in the dungeon and chained. The barbarians then whipped King Arthur until blood was flowing down his back. When he was whipped, King Arthur saw a peasant girl beside him getting some wine to cleanse his wounds. However the peasant girl was also a prisoner.

It was she. It was the girl that saved him from the Black Knight years ago.

"It's you," said King Arthur trembling.

"Yes, it's me. Lay down and rest. I'm going to cleanse your wounds now," said the girl named Marie. "When I was captured Sir Kay and Sir Ector heard me. They know where I am, but they are very far away."

"Are they sending a whole army to rescue us?" King Arthur asked curiously.

"I do not know," replied Maria.

Suddenly a loud BANG!!! echoed through the dungeon.

"Well, well, well. Who do we have here?" said a gigantic barbarian.

Maria and King Arthur were very quiet. They didn't dare make a sound because if they talked the barbarian would chop off their heads.

A few years passed. Sir Ector and Sir Kay were still searching for King Arthur and Maria.

One day a peasant came to one of the knights and said, "I have found King Arthur. He is in a barbarian's castle. I didn't dare save King Arthur because I knew that the barbarians would kill me/"

"Thank you for telling us. We will reward you kindly, peasant boy," said Sir Ector.

"You're welcome," said the peasant boy politely.

Sir Kay and Sir Ector set off the next day on a long days journey. First they went through the dark and gloomy forest.

When they were in the forest, they saw a few barbarians. The barbarians tried to strike them down. But Sir Ector sliced them down with his battle axe like slicing a piece of butter.

As the moon went up Sir Kay and Sir Ector started to feel hungry.

"Please forgive me Sir Ector. We don't have any food," said Sir Kay.

"How could you Sir Kay!!!" screamed Sir Ector at the top of his lungs. "We are going to DIE!!!"

"Calm down Sir Ector. There is a nearby village. We can ask them for food," said Sir Kay.

Sir Ector and Sir Kay had walked for miles. Finally, they reached the village. Some farmers in the fields saw the knights and offered some food and lodgings for them to rest.

When the knights were fast asleep, the farmers told all the farmers and peasants in town that two Knights of the Round Table were at his cottage. All the peasants and farmers gathered around the farmer's house.

"Wow, it's really them," said a farmer.

Suddenly everyone began clapping and cheering for them. Sir Ector and Sir Kay asked the farmer why they were cheering for them.

"This is the first time two Knights of the Round Table have come to this village," said the farmer.

"Thank you for the food and lodging. We will be leaving now," said Sir Ector.

After Sir Ector and Sir Kay left the village they saw a humongous castle a short distance away.

"I wonder whether that is the barbarians' castle?" asked Sir Kay.

"Of course it is. Don't you see the barbarian flag up there?" yelled Sir Ector.

Once they got near the castle, they saw two guards guarding the gate and fifty guards patrolling the castle.

"How are we going to get past all those guards?" asked Sir Kay.

"We can't," replied Sir Ector.

"I have an idea. We can ask the villagers to help us!" said Sir Kay excitedly.

"Great idea Sir Kay. Let's go!"

Sir Kay and Sir Ector ran like the wind back to the village. As a peasant boy walked across the village, he saw Sir Kay and Sir Ector.

"Hey guys. Look. It's Sir Kay and Sir Ector," called the peasant boy.

Everybody stopped in their tracks and looked at Sir Ector and Sir Kay.

"Wow, it is really them," said a farmer.

Just then a young peasant boy burst from the crowd.

"Ramon, at your service," said the young boy.

"Excuse me Ramon, but we need some of the villagers or farmers to fight for us," said Sir Kay.

"Fight who?" asked Ramon.

"The barbarians," answered Sir Ector.

"Of course, we have hated those people. They killed a lot of people in this village. We will be willing to send all our men," shouted Ramon.

"Get your men ready. We will leave before the sun comes down. We will then camp outside the barbarians' castle. We will attack the castle when the sun comes up," said Sir Ector.

Ramon immediately got the men and gave them their sickles, pitchforks, and knives. They then left the village and marched to the forest right outside the barbarians' castle.

"We will attack the castle tomorrow when the sun comes up," Sir Ector told the men.

The men started marching toward the castle. When they were outside the castle walls they went to get their battering ram.

"You people distract the barbarians and Sir Kay and I will go and get King Arthur," said Sir Ector.

BOOOOM!! The farmers banged the battering hammer against the brown drawbridge.

While the farmers were battering the brown drawbridge, Sir Kay and Sir Ector swept through the postern gate.

"Let's go to the dungeon. King Arthur will be there," Sir Ector said.

Luckily the keep wasn't heavily guarded but there were still some soldiers right outside. There were archers getting their bows ready.

"Be careful of the arrows Sir Kay. You go and get King Arthur. I will kill the guards," said Sir Ector confidently.

Sir Kay and Sir Ector struck the guards down and went through a secret passage way. They walked down some stairs and saw two doors.

"One says To Dungeon and the other says To Guards Room. Lets go to the dungeon,." said Sir Kay excitedly knowing that they would soon see King Arthur.

"You go rescue King Arthur and I'll distract the guards, understand?" said Sir Ector sternly.

"I understand, but…"

"We are running out of time. Just rescue King Arthur and come back here. Is that understood?" asked Sir Ector

"Yes Sir!" replied Sir Kay

"Let's move now,"

Sir Kay and Sir Ector ran in both directions. Sir Ector ran in the guard's room and killed everyone he saw.

Meanwhile, Sir Kay saw two guards right outside King Arthur's cell. Sir Kay ran in and struck both guards down. Sir Kay saw Sir Ector coming towards the dungeon. Suddenly, a gigantic barbarian stood right in front of Sir Ector.

"You're not going anywhere," said the barbarian.

He suddenly swung his battle axe behind him. Before he got a chance to swing it down, Sir Kay plunged his sword into the barbarian's back. When the barbarian fell on the damp floor, he shook the ground. Sir Kay checked the barbarian's pockets and found a key.

"Sir Kay, thanks for saving my life," thanked Sir Ector.

"It's my pleasure," replied Sir Kay

They walked and walked till they found which cell King Arthur was in. Sir Kay unlocked the doors.

"Are you alright?" asked Sir Ector.

"Thanks to Marie, I am," replied King Arthur.

"Marie is in this cell?" asked Sir Kay.

" She is over there," said King Arthur pointing at the corner.

"Marie, are you alright?" asked Sir Kay.

"I'm fine Sir Kay," said Marie.

"Let's head back to Camelot before dark," said Sir Ector.

King Arthur, Maria and the knights walked back to Camelot.

"I'll tell the farmers the war is over," said Sir Kay.

"Farmers were helping me?" asked King Arthur.

"Yes they were," replied Sir Ector.

"Invite them to my castle for a feast tomorrow," said King Arthur.

The next day, when the sun was up, all the farmers and peasants that helped in the war were right outside the castle.

"Open the gates and let them in, Sir Ector," said King Arthur.

"Yes King Arthur," replied Sir Ector.

The gates opened and the peasants rushed in the castle. The royal cooks prepared a feast. That was the greatest feast ever for King Arthur.

Mr. D's Class

THE WRITING PROCESS

While teaching third grade over the years I found many challenges in teaching them to write good stories. The biggest, however, was getting them to write a story that made sense. Their stories usually strung together a bunch of unrelated events that were often amusing but almost always confusing. I also found the story maps I was using not only didn't help, they actually seemed to make things worse. The story maps would ask for so much detail that kids ended up with a page filled with too many characters, events, problems, and miscellaneous details. By the time students began to write their stories they had a difficult time connecting so many ideas together; furthermore, once they began writing they usually ended up adding more characters and events, leaving out parts of their story map, and getting completely lost along the way.

I began simplifying my story maps and ended up with a very simple formula: Tell me your Big Problem and Big Resolution.

Almost every story has a big problem that sets events in motion and a big resolution that solves it. My favorite example is L. Frank Baum's The Wizard of Oz. When asked what is the big problem of this story, almost everyone will say the wicked witch. Although the witch is the antagonist and a really big problem, she wouldn't even have appeared in the book if it weren't for the Big Problem: Dorothy wanted to go home.* If Dorothy had landed in Munchkin Land and said, "Wow! This is much better than Kansas! I think I'll live here," then she would have never met the witch. She also wouldn't have met the Wizard to ask for a return home and the book would have had another name. When Dorothy killed the witch her troubles weren't over because she needed to go home to solve her Big Problem. The Big Resolution comes when she is safely back in Kansas.

Of course, it would be a very boring story if Dorothy had arrived, asked to go home, and then told by the good witch that she was wearing the answer. A story needs lots of obstacles along the way to make it exciting. So Dorothy meets three unusual friends, explores strange lands, and battles an evil witch. I have my students add two little problems and resolutions as obstacles to solving the Big Problem and Big Resolution.

When students understand the Big Problem that their story revolves around, they understand how to Resolve it. I have found it gives them a framework for their story. A clear idea of why their adventure began and how it will end.

*My Wizard of Oz example refers to the book, where Dorothy doesn't even meet the witch until the Wizard tells her to kill her. In the movie the witch immediately makes a nuisance of herself and won't leave poor Dorothy alone until she gets her ruby slippers. However, Dorothy's main goal remains the same: she wants to get home. Otherwise she would have asked the Wizard to kill the wicked old witch so she could keep her lovely slippers and live happily in Oz.

STORY MAP

Big Problem:

Little Problem number 1:

Little Resolution number 1:

Little Problem number 2:

Little Resolution number 2:

Big Resolution:

STUDENT FAIRY TALES

THE PRINCESS WHO WANTED TO BE A KNIGHT
By Lauren Kokos

One day there was a princess named Princess Storm. She wanted to be a knight really bad but girls weren't allowed to be knights because they didn't have the skills. Also boys were afraid that girls would be better than them.

She also had a kitten named Mitsu he had, white fur with ginger ears, and a short sturdy ginger tail, and blue eyes. Princess Storm and Mitsu played together, and even slept together. The princess loved Mitsu so much because when she was sad Mitsu would cheer her up.

One day Princess Storm was playing with Mitsu in the courtyard when she complained, "Mitsu how come I can't become a knight?"

"Meow. Meow. Meow." Answered Mitsu.

"Oh daughter!" yelled the king from the Great Hall.

"What!?!? asked Princess Storm

"Time for breakfast!" yelled back the king.

"OK! Well Mitsu maybe if I keep my hopes up I might become a knight." whispered Princess Storm to Mitsu.

Then she walked to the Great Hall for her daily breakfast. Following her breakfast she went upstairs in the Great Hall for her music class. The room was very big with many kinds of instruments such as a Shawn, a long and wooden instrument, like a flute, a Lizard, a black and wary instrument without any holes. There was also a Bladder Pipe made out of wood and animals bladder. A Lute, made out of wood and similar to a guitar. The one Princess Storm played was called the Psaltery. It was like a harp. There were two daily classes Princess Storm had to attend. Her teacher was Bertie.

"Ok Princess Storm start playing your Psaltery." asked Bertie.

"Ok Bertie." Answered Princess Storm.

Princess Storm was the only student in the music class.

Then she rode on Lightning, her horse, for awhile. After that she ate her lunch in the Great Hall "downstairs" Following that she went to the Chapel. "Church" The Chapel was very beautiful. It had, stained glass windows, a gold dove (means good luck), many pictures of Mary, Princess Storm went there every Sunday of her life. She never missed Chapel because if she did, she would have been considered a witch or a wizard. She would also be thrown into the river with crocodiles.

Then she had her dinner and went to sleep in the Great Bedchamber.

"Night mom. Night dad" whispered Princess Storm.

"Night Hunny." Whispered the King and Queen.

During the night Princess Storm sneaked out and went into the armory and took some armor and a sword.

"I wonder which armor will fit me?" wondered Princess Storm.

"This one will fit you perfectly Princess Storm." Said a man.

"Why thank you. Who are!?!? Screamed the princess.

"Who? Oh me?" asked the man.

"Yes! You! Answered the Princess Storm.

"I'm…Douglous. I take care of the horses and the armors.'"" said Douglous.

"Please don't tell that I'm going to go and be in the! shrieked Princess Storm.

"No. No. Don't worry I won't tell. Your just like your mother. She wanted to be in the contest too!" answered Douglous.

"So your not going to tell?" asked Princess Storm.
"Of course not."

"Thank you!"

So she hurried back to bed (with the armor) and went to sleep.

The next day Princess Storm got ready and set off for the contest in the courtyard. You probably wonder what the contest is about. First you shot some arrows after that two people get chosen and they do a joust. Whoever wins gets a kiss from the princess.

"I welcome you all to the contest! Our five contestants are….Sir Simon, Sir Arthur, Sir William, Sir Philip, and Sir…Sir…I don't know your name young man." asked the king.

Princess Storm thought quickly.

"Um…um…hum…Sir Stuart!" lied Princess Storm quickly.

"Ok you may…BEGIN! yelled the king.

ZOOM! ZANG! ZOOM! ZANG! ZOOM! Went the arrows.

"And…Sir Simon and Sir Stuart wins! And they get to go and have the joust!" shouted the King in excitement.

The horses were wearing expensive golden armor. The headpiece was classed the shaffron and for the back the main crinet.

"Get on your horses and Go!" said the King.

ZOOM! BANG! AAHH! BONK! ZOOM! On and on went the joust finally it was over.

"And the winner is….SIR STUART!" yelled the King.

"Thank you! Thank you!" said Princess Storm in her manly voice.

"You may kiss the princess" Wherever she is." Shouted the king.

"No need!" said Princess Storm.

And the king said why?

"Because sssmmmmmooooocccchhh." Said Princess Storm.

"Why did you kiss your own had Sir Stuart? Asked the king curiously.

"Because I am the princess!"

Everyone stared at Princess Storm (once she took off her helmet)

"I can't believe it." whispered the king. "I declare you CHAMPION!" screamed the king.

"Oh father do I get to be a knight?" asked Princess Storm.

"Of course! screamed the king.

So Princess Storm finally got to be a knight. And for Mitsu well…he got to be Princess Storm's squire. And for the Queen, well Princess Storm made her dream come true.

THE END

THE BRAVE KNIGHTS
Billy Zimmerman

One stormy day in a land faraway was a king. He was an evil king. He burned peoples' homes and took the people as slaves. He got more and more slaves and became more and more greedy. His name was Evil. But somewhere in a big cave lived brave knights. They wanted the slaves to be free. They had a plan. They all went in the cave to talk about the plan. "We must free the slaves," said one of the knights named Rocky.

"We must sacrifice our lives to kill King Evil and let the slaves be free," said the Black Knight. "Just follow my plan, Rocky." All the knights followed the Black Knight. They arrived at the gate of the Evil King's Castle. One of the King Evil's soldiers said, "Friend or enemy?"

"Friend," said Rocky.

The gate opened, and they saw King Evil sitting on his throne.

"What do you want?" asked King Evil.

"We want this!"

A knight quickly took out his arrow and shot it straight at the Evil King's head. Al the knights slashed, stabbed, and sliced King Evil's soldiers. Rocky opened the gate so the slaves could get out of the castle.

When the fight was over only one knight was standing. It was the old Black Knight. The slaves quickly followed the Black Knight to the cave. They were given food and water. All the slaves said, "God bless you brave knight!"

"You can call me Black Knight," said Black Knight.

"Can you free the other slaves from King Port?" asked one of the slaves.

"Who is King Port?" said the Black Knight.

"You don't know who he is?" said one of the slaves.

"Is he that guy who has the most slaves?" asked the Black Knight.

"Yes," said one of the slaves.

"Do you mean that you want me to free King Port's slaves," said Black Knight.

"Yes," said two of the slaves.

"But I need men to help me kill his men, free the slaves and lead them to the secret cave," said the Black Knight.

"I will help you," said one of the slaves

"Me too!" said a lot of the boy slaves.

"But, it's still not enough," said Black Knight.

"How about us?" said the slave girls.

"Give me a break, Girl are too weak to be knights," said all of the boys.

"That's not true, because one of the knights that freed you was a girl. It doesn't matter if they're not strong. What matters is how skilled they are," said the Black Knight. So they began to train. They trained for months, but there was one thing during this time that kept the slaves wondering. Why didn't the Black Knight ever take off his helmet? No one had ever seen his face. The one day the Black Knight said, "You guys stay here, I've got a surprise for you." With a big smile, he quickly went in the cave. The slaves were whispering about what the surprise might be.

Finally, the Black Knight brought out suits of armor, knives, spears, arrows, shields, daggers, horses and armor for the horses. Al of the boys and girls got ready for the battle. They made a plan to free the slaves and kill the king and his men.

When they arrived in front of the gate, one of the King Port's men said, "Friend or enemy?"

"Friend!" said the Black Knight. The gate opened, and they were in the castle's courtyard. King Port said, "What do you want, you stinky smelly knights?" All of the King Port's men started to laugh at them. Quickly one of the knights took out his arrow and shot King Port in the stomach. All the knights took out their arrows, swords, and spears and charged at King Port's men. Everyone fought hard. Black Knight opened the gate, and one of the knight led king Port's slaves to the secret cave. Finally, the war was over and just ten knights were standing. There was blood all over them and all over the castle. "Where is the Black Knight?" asked one of the knights.

"I'm right here," said the Black Knight. Black Knight had arrows in his chest and arms.

"We have to get a doctor!" screamed one of the knights.

"No! Leave me here," said the Black Knight.

"But we don't want you to die!" cried one of the knights.

"I will still die, but I have a secret for you."

He opened the front of his helmet, and all the knights were surprised.

"You're Knight Fox, the best knight!" said one of the knight.

Before the other knights could talk to Knight Fox, he was already dead. All the knights had tears running down their cheeks. Everything was silent. They buried him in the secret cave and everyone cried. Then they made a law; NO MORE SLAVES.

The Audition
By Karisa Sukamto

One sunny morning, a peasant named Bertie saw a poster saying:

We need someone to make the King laugh.
Auditions will be held at the castle.

"Wow! I want to get this job! I'm good looking man aren't I? I have bugs in my hair, a big bumpy nose, and yellow teeth. I have an organistrum, a type of instrument, and I can sing and dance." Bertie thought to himself, "But I don't have a clue where the castle is. I know. I'll ask another peasant."

The next day he proceeded to his friend's home. The house had a thatched roof, one window, straw mattresses, and farm animals eating scraps from the floor. "Hello Storm! Can you tell me where the castle is?"
"Sure, it's at Knights Avenue. Have a good day! Bye!"

"Bye Storm!" He ran off and went to Knights Avenue, but still could not find the castle. Then he saw another young man who had hair like silk, his face smooth and clean, his mouth shining in the sun, his nose smooth and straight, and his hands were big and clean too. Bertie asked, "Do you know where the castle is?"

"Sure I do. I'm going to the audition too. By the way, I'm Steamer." He said, glancing at the organistrum. "So you are?"

"I'm Bertie. So where's the castle?"

"What a weird name," Steamer said, grinding his teeth, trying to find a perfect aim of how to get his organistrum. The he quickly squeaked, "The castle is straight ahead!"

"Thanks!"

Steamer had already run away when Bertie realized his organistrum was gone! Steamer vanished in seconds and reached the castle hours before Bertie. Bertie sobbed, "What am I going to do without my organistrum?" Bertie thought and thought. "But I can still dance and sing like Sir Michael Jackson."

So he walked straight ahead through the dark forest, nervously thinking he would be too late for the audition and wouldn't get the job. After two hours of long and suffering, he finally reached the castle! It was big and made out of stone! Bertie walked in and then passed the portcullis. He marched through the courtyard where all the knights were practicing how to fight. Bertie passed them in amazement of how beautiful the horses were. He ran all the way to the second floor and to the great hall to dance for the King like Sir Jackson.

At the audition, he told the King, "I'm so sorry. I don't have an instrument to play. It was stolen when I was asking for directions from a guy named Steamer."

"Yeah right, but nice try. If you don't have an instrument, you will never get this job."

"But I can sing and dance like Sir Jackson."

"Fine, I'll give you a chance even though I doubt, you will get the job."

After he danced, he sang a legend about himself, it went: "It was love at first sniff, believe me, the princess smelled my breath and said, "Oh, it's stinky." She fainted right away, but I didn't care. I picked her up in my arms, and kicked her in the air!"

King Arthur was a short and stubby man with a long mustache. His nose was so big, Bertie could fit his whole body up his nostrils! "This is great! Well, I guess you are better than the other guy…fine, you're hired," King Arthur said laughing his head off!

"Really?"

"Yep! So start making me laugh!"

"Yippee!"

After he was done dancing, King Arthur told him to sit down and have a great time at the feast. He sat down feeling tempted to eat all the food. He was already drooling. There were steamed eggs, roasted chicken, boars, chicken, potatoes, and even ducks! They sat at wooden tables. The royalty sat on a different table in front of the peasants. While they were eating, there were jugglers and acrobats entertaining the people. When they were done with the feast, Bertie went in the kitchen. He saw that bread was baked in a wooden stove, and the boars would be roasted over the fire. There were tasters tasting all the food before the royalty and families ate. When he was done, he felt freedom because he never had so much food and happiness! As years passed, he became one of the King's favorite entertainers. And as for Steamer, he lived a bad life, because Bertie told King Arthur that Steamer stole his organistrum. He got punished for that.

0-595-23430-5